Harri Nykänen, born in Helsinki in 1953, was a well-known crime journalist before turning to fiction. He won the Clue Award for Finnish crime writing in 1990 and in 2001. His fiction exposes the local underworld through the eyes of the criminal, the terrorist and, most recently, from the point of view of an eccentric Helsinki police inspector called Ariel Kafka. This is the third in the Ariel Kafka series to appear in English. It follows on from the success of *Nights of Awe* and *Behind God's Back.*

D1014309

ALSO AVAILABLE FROM BITTER LEMON PRESS
BY HARRI NYKÄNEN

Nights of Awe

Behind God's Back

HOLY CEREMONY

Harri Nykänen

Translated by Kristian London

WITHDRAWN

BITTER LEMON PRESS
LONDON

BITTER LEMON PRESS

First published in the United Kingdom in 2018 by
Bitter Lemon Press, 47 Wilmington Square, London WC1X 0ET

www.bitterlemonpress.com

First published in Finnish as *Pyhä toimitus*
by Crime Time, Helsinki, 2011

© Harri Nykänen 2011
English translation © Kristian London, 2018

Bitter Lemon Press gratefully acknowledges the financial
assistance of FILI – Finnish Literature Exchange and
the support of the Arts Council of England.

  Supported using public funding by
**ARTS COUNCIL
ENGLAND**

English-language edition published by agreement with Harri
Nykänen and Elina Ahlback Literary Agency, Helsinki, Finland

A CIP record for this book is available from the British Library
ISBN 978–1–908524–898
eBook ISBN 978–1–908524–904

Typeset by Tetragon, London
Printed and bound by CPI Group (UK) Ltd, Croydon, CR0 4YY

1

I eyed the naked woman sprawled face down on the leather sofa, her back covered in a dense web of text. My subordinate, Detective Jari Oksanen, peered over my shoulder: "Someone's been watching too many American serial-killer movies." Then he read the words aloud: "*Evil is most dangerous when it dons the guise of holiness, and darkness cloaks itself in light...* Cuckoo."

It might have been the stick letters scrawled on the woman's skin or the suspense-movie ambiance, but I was getting the sense that the body on the sofa was merely bait, and I had just stepped into a trap from which it was too late to extricate myself. I froze and raised my arms in front of my face, as if shielding myself from an attack. Oksanen looked in surprise at my primitive reaction, passed down from ancestors who lived millennia ago.

I resorted to routine to recover: "Did you find out who owns the flat?"

"I don't know who the owner is, but the resident's name is Reijo Laurén. Forty-five, give or take. Lived at this address for a couple of years now. Not too chummy with the neighbors. I got a cell phone number, too, but I'm not getting through. Arja's checking out his info and background... What's that mean?"

Oksanen pointed at the small of the woman's back, which read *Ps 91:12*, and the similar sequences of letters and numbers underneath: *Matt 10:28, Matt 23:33*.

The first only took a second to register. We Jews know our Old Testament.

"I think it's from the Bible, a verse from the Psalms."

"Dang it. Just when I left my Bible at home," Oksanen said, patting his pockets.

Below the woman's right shoulder blade was a symbol resembling the mouth of a tunnel with a cross drawn inside it.

"Looks like an attic window," Oksanen said.

"Matt 10:28 means the Gospel of Saint Matthew..." I looked around and zeroed in on the bookshelf. A quick scan turned up what I was hoping to find: an old, black-backed, leather-bound family Bible. I yanked it from the shelf. The names of those who had passed on were recorded on the flyleaf: Axel, 12.9.1949; Voitto, 4.6.1954; Kirsti, 17.1.1962...

Flipping to the New Testament, I found what I was looking for: *And fear not them which kill the body, but are not able to kill the soul: but rather fear him which is able to destroy both soul and body in hell.* The passage had been underlined in pencil.

I glanced out the window when I heard the sound of a car. Vuorio, the medical examiner, was just parking his gleaming new Benz in the courtyard below.

The apartment in Helsinki's Töölö district wasn't your typical crime scene, but crime is no respecter of time or place. A generous thousand square feet, decorated in a style that spoke of the owner's affluence. The walls were hung with old representational art: landscapes, birds, bright spring snowfields and sun-dappled pine trunks, inlets with reedbeds and rowboats pulled up onshore. Some of the works might have even been worth something. The dark furniture and velvet upholstery conjured up images of an elderly person ensconced among jars of ointments, vials of pills, and photographs. There wasn't the tiniest hint of life in the place.

The setting conjured up a memory from nearly forty years ago. My father and I had gone to visit an old aunt who lay in lace sheets, white as death. The stale air and smell of her medication made me nauseous. When she tried to touch my cheek, I pulled back and hid behind my dad in horror. The next night I had a nightmare of her pale hands scrabbling around, searching for me. Later, when I saw the movie *Fiddler on the Roof*, it had a similar scene, where Tevye's deceased relatives come back from beyond the grave to put a stop to the marriage between his daughter and the butcher.

The living-room window faced westwards, onto the park-like courtyard, where the April lawn was still smeared to the ground from the weight of the past winter's snow. Although the earth was bare, a six-foot pile of the grimy stuff still stood at the rear of the yard, where it had been plowed up against the trash shed. It had been a long winter. The bleak, gray day and naked trees gave the landscape a particularly unnerving, melancholy cast. I almost started thinking all hope was lost and the wisest course of action would be to serenely lay myself down, fold my hands across my chest, and wait for liberating death to arrive.

"It doesn't seem like the apartment of someone that age," I remarked.

Oksanen looked around. He clearly found the exoticism of the scene titillating. I could picture him that evening at the café, telling his rally buddies what he'd just seen. In such circumstances, the laws on investigation confidentiality tended not to carry a whole lot of weight.

"Yeah, the decor looks more like a seventy-year-old's. Grandma used to have the same sort of armchair and bookshelf. Holy crap, and a painting almost exactly like that, too. A little bay with a boat on the shore." Oksanen stared at the painting, entranced by his feeling of déjà vu. "One of the neighbors told me Laurén inherited the flat. Pretty weird he didn't bother heading out to IKEA to pick up some newer furniture. That TV is genuine '70s vintage, too."

I opened the ventilation window; I needed fresh air. I wouldn't have lasted twenty-four hours in the apartment without losing my mind.

The door swung open and I saw Vuorio enter, huffing and purposefully swinging his satchel. He nodded as he passed us, and braked when he reached the deceased's head. The medical examiner squatted down, stared at the woman's face for a moment, surveyed her body from head to toe, and let his fingers graze a pea-sized mole on her shoulder. Then he stood.

"This is one for the memoirs," he said, still breathing heavily from his climb. Vuorio was tremendously over-weight. His hobby was hunting big game in Africa, but imagining him taking aim at a buffalo or a leopard on the savannah was like picturing Luciano Pavarotti scaling the south face of Mount Everest.

Vuorio's comment perplexed me, because it seemed like he hadn't paid the slightest attention to the writing on the woman's skin.

"What?"

"For the first time in my career, the same person has been killed twice... or, to be exact, not killed, but killed herself twice... although there wasn't any writing on the body then." He paused, then continued, "This woman was found dead in her apartment yesterday. Had downed a vial of sedatives. I went to the scene myself. We brought her in for an autopsy, but for some reason she's here now... And I know I'm not mistaken," Vuorio said, anticipating my next question.

I moved on to the following one: "Where did she live?"

"Konala. Her name is Roosa Nevala. Sister came in to ID her. Had left a note; no indications of a crime. Takamäki's team is handling it, in case you're interested. According to the sister, Roosa had psychiatric problems, had been an inpatient for a long time but had gotten a place at a group home. Not everyone is built for this life, even when it's softened by meds."

"How can you be so sure it's her?" Oksanen asked. "She's lying on her stomach."

"Even twins don't have identical birthmarks." Vuorio indicated the pinky-tip-sized birthmark on the left shoulder, then the left hand. "Three horizontal slash marks on the left wrist, operation scar behind the left knee, same face, hair, body type, age. If either of you wants to place a bet, I accept. What I'm saying is you have a pretty rare case here, but whether it's a crime, now that's a different matter. Doesn't look like necrophilia; I can say that with relative confidence."

I considered Vuorio's words and decided he was right. The removal of a body from medical examiner custody was at most theft, or violation of the sanctity of the grave. Neither fell under the purview of the Violent Crimes Unit. More than anything, it sounded like the case belonged in the hands of a competent psychiatrist.

"I'd still be interested in finding out what the motive is," Oksanen said, almost disappointed. I uncharitably reflected that the incident was sure to be of interest to the media, and what interested the media also interested Oksanen.

Vuorio went on. "I'm thinking it has to do with the message this poor girl appears to have ended up being the notepad for. The message is pretty heavy-duty, so the ramifications are presumably of the same caliber. Which means I wouldn't be surprised if this case eventually ended up in your hands anyway."

"What ramifications?" I asked.

"I doubt whoever stole the body and wrote that on it did it on a whim. You don't just stroll into our unit and wheel out the first body you see. The writing refers to something."

"The Bible?" I suggested.

Vuorio frowned and looked past me. "*For he shall give his angels charge over thee, to keep thee in all thy ways... Thou shalt tread upon the lion and adder: the young lion and the dragon shalt thou trample under feet...* Psalm 91. One of the best known, which is why I remember it too. We had to memorize it at confirmation camp. It has a lot of verses, and I don't remember anything close to all of them. In any event, it strikes me that whoever wrote this has a pretty big chip on his shoulder about something."

"How would Laurén have gotten the body out of your facility, if it *is* him? Laurén is the owner of the flat."

"Can't say. We're not exactly the Bank of Finland; up until now none of our clients have been stolen for use in secret voodoo rituals. My guess is a staff member helped, or else the thief worked for us at some point and knows his way around."

"You guys have surveillance cameras, don't you?"

"Everywhere you turn. The doors are equipped with alarms, too. It's unlikely the bodysnatcher was working alone. Just carrying the body up here to – what is this, the third floor? – would have taken significant strength. It must have been rolled up inside a rug or something similar. But I'd still be asking *why* rather than *how*. It says quite a lot that he was prepared to put his name and his future on the line. Why this sort of MO, which brands him as good as a pervert? Why not a nice, tidy letter? How did you guys find out about this?"

Our arrival on the scene had been prompted by an anonymous tip called into the general emergency line, and I told Vuorio so.

"So I presumed. In other words, I'm guessing this is a prelude to something bigger. It makes me think this is the first move in some sort of game. This corpse here is the first sacrificed pawn."

Vuorio's attitude toward cases could typically be described as disinterested; he only communicated as much as his job required. Now he seemed downright enthusiastic, as if he were participating in some role-playing game, or solving a brain-teaser.

"Go talk with the neighbors; ask them if they've seen anything," I ordered Oksanen.

"Why, if this isn't even our case?"

"For now it is. We've already dragged ourselves all the way over here, so we're not leaving until our work is done."

Oksanen clearly begged to differ, but I ignored him. I turned my back and heard him trudging towards the door.

Before I had time to process Vuorio's ideas, my phone vibrated, announcing an incoming call. I glanced at the number. It was Arja Stenman, one of my subordinates. I stepped over to the window. "What is it?"

"I found all sorts of stuff on Laurén. Owns the flat; inherited it from his aunt three years ago, studied cello at the Sibelius Academy, had a side gig as a member of a heavy metal band called Holy Night, convicted of narcotics possession and unlawful intimidation, lived in Tibet for a few years, divorced, one child, restraining order, spent almost a year at the psychiatric hospital in

Kellokoski after a psychotic episode. Numerous employers within the past five years; last worked at a funeral home. The narcotics conviction is so old it was already removed from the register."

"We were a little too hasty. This isn't one of ours. The woman wasn't killed."

"What do you mean?"

I gave her the run-down.

"Doesn't matter; we have to find Laurén, if for no other reason than to get him psychiatric treatment," Stenman said. "I spoke with the sister of the deceased. According to her, Roosa was dating a man who could well be Laurén. Said the guy clearly had psychological problems that had a negative impact on her sister."

"Put out an APB on him. And while you're at it, check whether the medical examiner was a client of Laurén's former employer, that funeral home. We'll see who this case actually belongs to."

"Ari." Vuorio was standing next to the corpse, stout as a snowman. I tried to imagine him as the great white hunter, in sweat-stained khakis and a wide-brimmed Stetson, with little success. On the other hand, I had no trouble picturing him in a creaking rattan chair on the terrace of a colonial manor, sipping a gin and tonic or a mojito. "Come take a look at this."

Vuorio had rolled the corpse on its side, revealing an envelope that had been hidden under its breast. I bent over to see the name printed on the white paper:

Ariel Kafka.

2

I opened the envelope, making sure not to leave any prints on it. The sole contents were a yellowed newspaper clipping and the following note, written on a slip of paper:

This is not the beginning of my work, nor is it the end. There are five evil dragons and three good angels, who together form the Sword of God the Good. At the beginning of time, the dragons were strong, but goodness gathers strength over the years as we approach the end of the days of wickedness and the great cleansing. One dragon has been cast into darkness and filth, another burned with a purifying flame. But the battle will not be won until the most powerful dragon has been slain and cast into the fires of perdition. Only then will the Holy Ceremony come to its conclusion.

The Adorner of the Sacred Vault

The headline on the clipping read *Maintenance man found dead in Kouvola septic tank.* According to the date penciled on it, the article was from a 2008 issue of the *Kouvola Sanomat.* The story was about a maintenance man named Leo Anteroinen, born in 1951, who had been found brutally murdered in his septic tank. He was discovered by a friend who had been trying to reach him and eventually came by his home looking for him. The hatch to the tank had been left cracked.

After reading the clipping, I called Stenman and asked her to look up what she could find on the Kouvola murder.

Vuorio had finished his work and walked up to me. "What was in the letter?" He was sworn to confidentiality, so I let him read the message, which he handled as carefully as I had. "This is starting to feel as mystical as *The Lord of the Rings*. Any idea why your name was on the envelope?"

"Maybe he saw it in the paper and it stuck in his mind."

"How did he know you'd be the one called to the scene?"

"He probably didn't. But he knew it would be passed on to me anyway."

"Based on the letter, it sounds like he wants you specifically to do the investigating, and that there's some link to the incident mentioned in the clipping… well, there's no point assuming."

"I asked Stenman to get the preliminary investigation records."

"I doubt our corpse here has anything to do with any of this; it was such a clear suicide. I get the sense that the perpetrator is trying to draw the attention of the police – meaning you – to himself and get them to take him seriously. The letter reinforces my hunch."

Oksanen returned from making the rounds of the neighbors.

"The upstairs neighbor saw two men, one of whom was Laurén, carrying a rolled-up rug from the courtyard into the stairwell. Didn't recognize the other guy. Middle-aged, beanie, parka. The vehicle was a light-colored van. Female witness, didn't recognize the make." Oksanen's tone was almost disparaging. For him, identifying cars was a fundamental element of cultural literacy.

"I'm guessing my presence is no longer required," Vuorio said.

I sensed that my presence was no longer required either, and so I joined Vuorio and Oksanen in subjecting ourselves to the dispiriting effect of the hazy spring weather. In overly large doses, it brought out self-destructive tendencies. Vuorio climbed into his brand-new steel-blue Benz wagon. Oksanen eyed it a little enviously, as all we had at our disposal was an unmarked police clunker.

"I can see you have an eye for quality."

"A poor man can't afford to be cheap," Vuorio replied, stiffly lowering himself behind the wheel.

Vuorio was anything but poor. There was no way he could be, since his family owned twelve thousand acres of forest, a couple of Helsinki apartment buildings, and stocks and shares of every description.

"If the case ends up staying in our hands, I'll come out tomorrow to have a look around," I said.

Vuorio nodded and sped off.

"You mind dropping me off on Mansku?" Oksanen asked.

I started the car and followed Vuorio. He was already turning north.

"He's going way over the speed limit. You wouldn't think he had it in him," Oksanen said admiringly. "Where do these nutjobs come from? I'm talking about whoever snatched that body. Wandering around, when they should be locked up in the loony bin. The streets are full of them these days. Carrying a body home: what sense does that make?"

"Some sort, evidently."

"Sense is overrated."

I found myself agreeing with what Vuorio had said at the scene: this wasn't the work of some random lunatic. Everything had a point and a purpose, which was substantiated by the letter.

Oksanen continued: "I wouldn't bet on it. I can't think of any reason why someone would nab a body, except to perv on it, or else he's just off his rocker… drop me off at that bus stop up there. I need to pick up my car from the garage."

It seemed like Oksanen's car was in the shop more than it was on the road. Not that it was your average set of wheels: it was a six-cylinder Audi with an engine that violated all EU noise limits. It had been tuned, widened, lightened, and souped up. The Eläintarha gas station stayed in business thanks in large part to Oksanen's fuel purchases.

"Now?"

"I promised to be there by four."

I glanced at the clock on the dash: 3:22.

"It's in Pitäjänmäki. It's not like we have anything else going today, do we?" In Oksanen-speak, this meant he wouldn't be coming back into the office.

I found a spot to pull over. Oksanen popped his door open and said, one foot already out of the car: "Arja and I agreed that she can stay late tonight if you need someone to pull OT."

I edged forward to make room for the bus that appeared for Oksanen as if by magic. He waved as he sprinted for its front door.

I passed the sports hall, and it brought back memories. We used to play there when I was on the Makkabi table tennis team; the Makkabi was the Helsinki Jewish community's athletic club. I had played seriously for over five years. I didn't quit until shortly before my military service. I liked table tennis because I was good at it; it was the only sport I was better at than my big brother Eli. Eli remembered this and had recently asked me to head up the team, which had dwindled into nonexistence. Trendier sports had taken its place. The suggestion was appealing, as I'd let myself get out of shape. Maybe I could get some play in again as coach.

It was so late that I probably would have just headed home if I hadn't been driving a vehicle signed out from the HQ garage. It was a Ford Focus with shocks that rattled like castanets down Helsinki's cobblestone streets.

Our premises at VCU, the Violent Crimes Unit, looked as temporary as they were. The major renovation at HQ was supposed to be finished by fall. One could always hope.

I popped into Stenman's office. She had stayed late to do some digging into Laurén's background. I wanted to get an update on some other things, too. I sat down and waited for her to get off the phone.

"What'd you find out?"

"No sign of Laurén yet. Other than that, nothing earth-shattering, but it smells like this could become a time-consuming case. Where do you want me to start?"

"Just give me the relevant stuff."

I had come to trust Stenman's sense of relevance much more than mine. She was one of the investigators I relied on most, alongside Simolin, who was in Canada at the moment familiarizing himself with the local Indian tribes. North American Indians were a hobby for him the same way cycling or stamp collecting was for someone else, or sponsored motorsports were for Oksanen.

Stenman had used her time efficiently: "Reijo 'Reka' Laurén was born in Vaasa in 1962. Dad was a second-generation pharmacist, in other words the local upper crust, top of the municipal tax lists. Reijo was an only child. Attended boarding schools until college. Then he moved to Helsinki to study at the Sibelius Academy. Applied himself at first, but since the old man was footing the bill, gradually got used to a pretty lax pace. Eventually school fell by the wayside altogether, after he founded a band with some fellow students. Drug use entered the picture, which apparently didn't suit him, because it wasn't long before he was in inpatient treatment with psychological problems. After being released from the halfway house, he married a fellow student. They had one child, who's now seventeen. Divorced after ten years together. Laurén also had a falling-out with the old man when the latter stopped doling out cash. But at that point his aunt conveniently died, and Laurén inherited the apartment, money, and stocks. Convicted on one count of narcotics possession. That's it."

"So you talked with the ex-wife?"

"Briefly. They're not in contact anymore. Laurén is paying his child support these days, too, so she has no reason to be nagging him about that. He sees the kid pretty infrequently."

"Set up a meeting with her for tomorrow. You don't just do something like this out of the blue. He must have been brooding about something for years that led to the act itself. I'd be surprised if the wife is completely clueless as to what's going on. Just the opposite; she may feel like she's heard all about Laurén's intentions to the point of boredom. Any friends?"

"According to the wife, he kept in touch with a couple of buddies from high school, but she never met them and doesn't remember their names. I get the impression she wasn't too interested in her husband's affairs, not then and not now."

I reflected that quite a few wives were like that, adding, "Someone probably helped him move the body from the medical examiner's to the apartment. The neighbor said she saw Laurén carrying a rolled-up rug in the stairwell with another man, roughly the same age."

"That's all I have for now. I can continue tomorrow."

"What about the septic tank thing in Kouvola?"

"Anteroinen was from Kurikka. He attended vocational school and worked a bunch of places around the country as a custodian and a maintenance man, until he finally found the job in Kouvola, at a wholesaler's warehouse. Unmarried. I printed out the material from the preliminary investigation. Lead investigator was Lieutenant Pohtola, but he's dead. The detective working the case was Rimpelä, who's with the Oulu PD these days." As I reached across to receive the stack of information Stenman had put together, I caught a whiff of her expensive perfume. I had the momentary urge to lower my head into her lap.

I returned to my office to call Rimpelä. He was already home; I could hear the sounds of a children's television show in the background. I introduced myself.

"Two years back you investigated a case in Kouvola where a maintenance man was drowned in a septic tank."

"Yeah, but we never solved it... we had suspicions, but that's as far as it got. What is it about it that interests you?"

"Routine check. What suspicions?"

"Helsinki PD, was that it, and Kafka?"

"Yeah. Detective Kafka from the VCU," I said for the second time.

"I've heard your name."

"I have the material from the preliminary investigation, but I'd like to talk with you first. You mentioned something about suspicions."

"I'm in kind of a rush. I'm supposed to take my boy to swimming lessons."

"All I need are the basics. After that I'll read through the material and get back to you if necessary."

"Well, if you don't need more than a few minutes. What I meant was we actually had some potential motives, but no suspects per se. Didn't arrest or detain anyone. It was a tricky case all around. Ran into dead ends everywhere we turned. We did what we could. The boys from the Bureau even came in to have a look, but they couldn't squeeze any more out of it than we could. Left me thinking they're a little overrated."

"What were the motives?"

"Property crimes. This Anteroinen was a maintenance man at an electronics wholesaler, and it turned out there had been a massive series of thefts, had been going on for years. Hundreds of thousands of euros' worth of goods had vanished, all told. Apparently he got into an argument with his thief buddies over dividing up the take. There were some pretty hard-boiled guys involved... Some of the stolen goods had turned up at Anteroinen's cabin, and he was facing charges for them."

"But you guys didn't find any evidence of a connection between the crimes and the murder?"

"Just a few whispers from the underworld, which all supported the notion that it hadn't been a settling of scores between thieves. Why would Helsinki be interested in this case?"

"We're checking up on a tip. Was there anything unusual about the body?"

"Plenty. Anteroinen had been roughed up bad. Burn marks on the arms and torso. Some sort of flammable liquid had been poured over him and ignited. We didn't ever release that to the general public. After that, he was drowned in his own shit. Pretty unpleasant way to die."

"Did you notice any signs, drawings?"

"Oh, yeah. I forgot. We didn't tell anyone that, either, for investigative reasons, and we're not telling anyone now, either. Some sort of arch had been incised into his back, with a cross inside."

"Did you guys try to figure out what it meant?"

"Of course, but we came up empty-handed. We settled on a diversion the perp used to try and get us to believe that it was a ritual murder by some Holy Rollers."

"One last thing. Did the name Reijo Laurén come up in any way during the investigation?"

"Not that I can recall, no. I'm pretty sure about that."

Superintendent Huovinen still possessed a certain panache from his youthful days as a male model. His matching blue-and-gray sport coat, striped shirt, and tie fit to a T, as if he were on a catwalk, not in the drab bureaucratic offices at police HQ. For a cop, Huovinen was almost inappropriately stylish, some even thought handsome. A few years after we graduated from the police academy, he and I had been out with our girlfriends at the time, and my companion – I don't even remember her name – couldn't take her eyes off him all night. He had some silver at his temples now, but he was one of those guys it worked for. I was almost jealous. My own hair was starting to thin at the crown, with splotches of gray here and there. Because Huovinen was the head of the VCU in addition to being a smooth public speaker, he was a frequent presence on television. No wonder two political parties had asked him to join and put himself forward as a candidate in the upcoming elections. Huovinen's star was on the rise. He was widely considered a good bet to replace the deputy police chief, who was approaching retirement age.

I sat in my superior's bare-bones office, which faced westwards towards the evening sun, reporting on the envelope addressed to me and the theft of the body. He listened attentively. He had always been a good listener.

"I've never heard anything like that before," he said, nonplussed.

I conceded that I hadn't either.

"And there's no sign of the perpetrator?"

"We're looking for him now. Or rather for Reijo Laurén, the owner of the flat, who's in all likelihood the perp and the author of the letter."

"Do you think he's also behind the killing in Kouvola?"

"It's worth looking into."

"Sounds like he considers himself some sort of avenging angel. What was he the adorner of, again?" Huovinen asked.

"The Adorner of the Sacred Vault."

"Sounds like some Freemason title."

"It's not. I googled it."

"Plus he's hinting that his work isn't finished yet. What work? Killing?"

"That's what it seems like. 'The dragon to be slain' apparently refers to someone he considers evil. Which would imply that the maintenance man was one of the already-slain evil dragons."

"So some sort of secret society. He mentions three angels – in other words, there are three of them – and that they intend on killing at least one more person'."

"If you ask me, the one Laurén poses the most danger to is himself."

"Does he have any family?"

"An ex-wife who hasn't heard a peep from him in at least a year. Laurén lived in a flat he inherited from his aunt. The aunt was his last remaining relative. Arja found out that he had come into a substantial sum of money at the same time, and a nice chunk of stocks. There was plenty for him to live off."

"What do you make of the Bible passages?"

"He might be communicating that he isn't afraid of anyone and will emerge victorious. From what? Whatever it is, it's presumably of his own imagining. That also has a paranoid tinge to it."

"Or not. Maybe it really was a declaration of war," said Huovinen.

"Pretty hard to believe."

"He managed to get his hands on the body without getting caught, brought it up to the apartment, and called it in even though he knew that he would put the police on his tail. The fact that he's crazy doesn't make him stupid. And the fact that he convinced someone to help him move the body points to careful planning. Maybe there *are* three of them, after all."

Huovinen was such a busy man I was surprised he was prepared to sacrifice his time to this unusual but ultimately pretty insignificant case. Maybe he just wanted a moment's relief from the tedium of administration. We'd known each other going back to our days at the police academy, so we had no trouble chatting without the usual subordinate–superior stiffness.

"War is a big word. War against what?" I said.

"You tell me."

"Based on what Arja pulled up, he doesn't seem like the sort of crazy person who's living in a delusional world, more like the type for whom this world is too tough and who needs the occasional stint in in-treatment to calm down. Which often points to childhood trauma and…"

I couldn't help but think then of my sister Hanna, who committed suicide at the age of 28. Her life been changed irreversibly in the heart of Jerusalem, by a bomb that exploded at an outdoor café. Her friends' bloodied and mutilated bodies haunted her for the rest of her brief life. In the end, she could only find one way to rid herself of them. But two-cent psychologizing wasn't my field, so I let it go. I was an amateur, and so was Huovinen.

"This is a case that doesn't really belong to anyone, so we could go ahead and take it, seeing as how we've already begun. Go through the preliminary investigation material for the Kouvola case, then we can take another look. You go ahead and do it if Laurén wants you to so badly. Apparently something about your background appeals to his sick logic. Maybe he'll get in touch again one way or another and tell you more. And nothing to the papers yet. We have to assume that Laurén is at least partially of unsound mind."

I paused for a moment to consider whether I should refuse or be pleased. I leaned towards the latter; I had to admit that, in spite of myself, the case intrigued me.

Huovinen misinterpreted my hesitation. "Or don't you want to?"

"No, I do."

3

Huovinen's wish to keep the bodysnatching out of the press didn't come true. It was in the next day's *Ilta-Sanomat*. Someone had leaked like a sieve. The article reported that the body of a woman who had committed suicide had been stolen from the medical examiner's office and transported to an apartment in Töölö. The paper even knew about the light-colored van. Maybe the reporter had chatted up the same neighbor as Oksanen. At least there was no mention of the writing on the body; that meant the leaker wasn't one of ours. That still left plenty of alternatives: someone from the medical examiner's staff, a neighbor, a family member...

On an impulse, I called Jyri Moisio, the crime reporter who had written the story. I had met him once, at the press conference for a different case, but didn't know him well. I had always tried to keep my distance from reporters.

"I know you guys have to protect your sources, and I'm not interested in who spilled the story, other than in investigative terms. I think it's possible that the person who tipped you guys off is the same individual who stole the body."

"What makes you think that?"

"We found the body thanks to an anonymous tip, too."

I could practically hear Moisio's crime-reporter brain clicking. "I can tell you this much: your theory isn't out of the question."

"So the information didn't come from any of the authorities or some similar source?"

"I guess I can tell you that the caller was anonymous. Of course, we used our own sources to check out the story."

The reporter tried to take advantage of the situation and pry further details out of me, but I'd gotten what I wanted and ended the call.

I started browsing through the Anteroinen paperwork. The photos of the crime scene were chilling. Anteroinen lived in a house that was a little way outside Kouvola, so the killer or killers had been able to take their time. The burning had taken place in the garage. After that, Anteroinen had been dragged out alive and thrown into a septic tank no more than a few hundred gallons in size. The cause of death was suffocation. I read the half-dozen interrogation reports Rimpelä had written up, but there was nothing interesting in them. For such a gruesome case, they were surprisingly tame. As if the entire incident hadn't had the least effect on the investigator.

The medical examiner's office was tucked away in a funny little cul-de-sac closely shaved on either side by two of the city's main traffic corridors. I parked in the space reserved for police and funeral-home vehicles and climbed the stairs to the main entrance. At the corner of the building, I made a note of three surveillance cameras pointing in different directions.

I announced my business to the receptionist. She called Vuorio.

"He'll be up in just a minute. You can wait over there." She nodded at a cluster of pale-blue chairs by the window, and I accepted her offer.

My phone rang; it was Huovinen. He got right down to business: "Where are you?"

"Medical examiner's. I'm trying to figure out how Nevala's body made it out."

"Good. Come see me when you get back."

"Something out of the ordinary?"

"Yes."

"Tell me."

"There will be plenty of time when you're back. Solve the mystery of the stolen body first."

I saw Vuorio walk into the lobby. In his lab coat, he would have passed for a good-natured pediatrician. After we shook hands, he started to lead me into the building, although I knew my way.

"As you can see, all the doors are equipped with alarms that will alert the security company if the door stays open too long," he explained. Then he pulled out his keychain and showed me his ID card. "You have to have one of these to be able to move around in here, and your movements are tracked by the security system."

"Who was on duty the other night?"

Vuorio chuckled. "I was. And I didn't see or hear anything. I opened up a vagrant who had died of a cerebral hemorrhage, and then I went to sleep in my office. I woke up around four, plugged my way through about an hour's worth of paperwork, then went online and reserved a week at a lodge in Estonia. I'm headed there this fall to hunt wild boar. My guess is the body was removed earlier in the evening. If I were you, I'd check with the security company."

"Are there many other alternatives?"

"Such as?"

"Current or former employees? Janitors, for instance. One of them could have stolen the key. Maybe it was the cleaning lady's boyfriend. But back to that night: I suppose there were others here, aside from you?"

"Nope. The prep guy went home once he finished laying the groundwork. We're on a budget, just like all government agencies. Overtime is expensive. If we get a drunk driver or a suspected drug user, we call in a chemist."

Vuorio pushed the door to his office wide and held it open for me. His desk was heaped with stacks of papers, various forms, instruments, books, pizza boxes, and paper cups. It was pure chaos. A gray armoire stood behind the desk. On the wall hung photographs of Vuorio during high-caliber hunting trips to the ends of the earth: Africa, Russia, Estonia, Lapland. He enjoyed traipsing about the great outdoors, although you'd never know it from his appearance. An oil painting in blue tones hung across from the desk, a sharp contrast to all the masculine paraphernalia. It was of a woman, fortyish, foreign-looking. I knew the subject was Vuorio's deceased wife. She had died from cancer over ten years earlier.

The medical examiner waved a coffee mug he had unearthed from the mountains of papers. "Should I make us some coffee?"

"No thanks. Where are the surveillance camera tapes?"

"At the security company, or at least I think so. Pretty interesting case if it turns out someone came in using their keys."

"Are you sure there's no way to circumvent the security system to get into the building?"

"You'll have to ask the lads from the security company."

"How often do they come here?"

"Only as often as necessary, in other words if the alarm system indicates something's wrong. This isn't one of those sites they visit every night. There's nothing here of interest to the guards, except maybe the ethanol."

"Ever have false alarms?"

"Apparently not very often, because I've never seen or heard of one."

"Where was the body?"

"In the morgue."

I tried to remember where it was located.

Vuorio seemed to read my mind. "Two floors down. You can access it directly from the loading ramp. There are other ways of exiting the building from the morgue, too."

"If the body was moved from the morgue on a stretcher, it would have been left somewhere. Did anyone report anything like that, finding a stretcher outside?"

"Good thinking. No, at least not me. I went home in the morning, slept, and came back to work. I have to take a couple more years of this butcher shop. You can bet your behind I won't be missing this job once I retire… Do you want to have a look around the morgue?"

"I'd love to."

I wondered at my choice of words. There were some things I loved; spending time in a room of bodies in steel drawers wasn't one of them. But it had to be done.

Vuorio called the elevator, which we rode down two floors. Then there was a bit more trudging down echoing corridors until we arrived at our destination.

The space was just like the ones everyone has seen on foreign cop shows, the ones where they show a body lying under a sheet with a name tag looped around the toe. The room was cold, and smelled of disinfectant and rancid meat. An entire wall was nothing but stainless-steel lockers.

Vuorio studied a folder on the desk and stepped right over to one of the steel doors.

"Here's our little runaway," he said, yanking it open.

He stood there staring at the drawer that had popped out. I saw the same thing he did.

The locker was empty.

4

When I conveyed the information that Roosa Nevala's body was missing again, Huovinen's response was brief: "Unbelievable."

Which was a lot, coming from him. With over twenty years on the force under his belt, he knew almost anything was possible.

"Vuorio suspects it was never even returned."

"The guys from the funeral home, huh?"

"Yeah. When we left Töölö, we just left a patrol behind. They probably wouldn't ask too many questions if two guys in lab coats showed up with a stretcher and a body bag to do a pickup."

"Maybe. Find out which patrol turned over the body." Huovinen scratched the underside of his chin. "If the first theft didn't make any sense, this makes even less, or if it does, it's some sort of sense that's beyond me."

"Yeah, this corpse recycling is a total mystery to me, too."

"If this leaks to that reporter punk, I'm going to turn the whole PD upside down until I find out who did it."

I shared my suspicions that the leak had come from outside, potentially from Laurén himself.

"I have to hand it to him, he's cooking up a real mess. If we could grasp even a tiny bit of what he's thinking, we would know what to anticipate. This is an unusually contradictory case, Ari. When it comes down to it, simple theft of a body, even twice over, isn't much of a crime. If, on the other hand, it's an omen of something more serious to come, we should try and prevent it. But you and I aren't mind readers. I guess we can't do much more than try and figure out how the body was stolen."

"There was something else you wanted to talk about, too," I reminded him.

"Yeah, that's a shitty piece of business, too. It's about Oksanen."

Huovinen took a letter from a locked desk drawer and passed it to me. I sat in my familiar spot. The letter was brief, but the gist was clear. The author purported to be the recently retired secretary of the CEO of a well-known auto parts business.

For years now, in my capacity at work I have been forced to watch a detective named Jari Oksanen exploit his position to extort discounts or free parts for his rally car. My impression is that he has something he's using to blackmail Mr. Berg, the CEO, or at least threatening to do so. I feel sorry for Mr. Berg, because he's quite nice, a real old-fashioned gentleman. I'm certain the value of these extorted handouts totals thousands of euros. Oksanen was occasionally accompanied by a member of police command from the ministry; I don't recall the name. I've never dared to go public with this matter, but now that I've retired, I feel it is my duty. Detective Oksanen will of course claim that it's part of a sponsorship arrangement, but you can rest assured that is not the case. I have heard Mr. Berg speak about it in dismayed tones on numerous occasions. You are free to use my name, because I know anonymous tips are not held in very high regard.

They say a crow never pecks out another crow's eyes, but I hope you get to the bottom of this and Detective Oksanen is called to account. If not, I will turn to the media.

Saimi Vartiainen

The letter also included Ms. Vartiainen's phone number and address.

It was a straightforward matter. Either the information was accurate or it wasn't. There was no question it needed looking into.

"Everyone knows about Oksanen's rallying, so unfortunately the letter has the veneer of credibility. It looks bad," Huovinen said. "What do you think?"

It's not always easy being a superior, especially when you have to be loyal and critical at the same time.

"We have to investigate."

"Of course… do you happen to know who Oksanen's co-driver is?"

I scoured my memory. Oksanen's hobby held zero interest for me, but some of it couldn't help but stick. I recalled the police rally team's victorious pose after the competition in Poland, the photo published in *PD* magazine. It also hung on the wall of Oksanen's office, along with memorabilia from other wins.

"Goddammit! It's Kalliola!"

Arto Kalliola was the deputy national police commissioner from the Ministry of the Interior.

"They drive together, so he's at risk of being accused of benefiting from Oksanen's dealings. He probably doesn't know anything about Oksanen's shenanigans, but that's hard to prove. If it looks shady, it *is* shady."

Huovinen sounded frustrated. I wasn't sure if it was because of what Oksanen had done, or the fact that Oksanen had gotten Kalliola mixed up in his dirty business. The rules on internal investigations mandated that a police officer couldn't investigate a colleague working in the same municipality of any suspected crimes. In Oksanen's case, that meant the investigation would presumably be turned over to the Espoo PD, and the investigation would be led by someone appointed by the prosecutor general's office.

Once I had time to think about it, I started feeling guilty. I had been Oksanen's superior and knew all about his expensive hobby, but I hadn't bothered to think how he financed it. On the other hand, what was I supposed to do? It's not like he would have confessed to me that he was wheedling or demanding discounts from a car-parts supplier. In addition to the guilt, I felt a creeping schadenfreude. Oksanen's endless tinkering, branded jackets, and prize-podium photos had been getting on my nerves for a long time, especially since there was no question they ate into his working hours. I had tried not to show my frustration, because everyone was free to have whatever hobbies they wanted, as long as they weren't illegal – a line we were fast approaching.

"How should we proceed?" I asked Huovinen.

"It's best to do things by the book. As his closest superior, you have a word with him first. After that we'll talk to him together. If there's the slightest cause for suspicion, we'll turn it over to the prosecutor."

I headed for my office, and of course just then Oksanen trudged down the corridor towards me in his blue branded jacket, still looking groggy even though it was almost ten. I looked at my watch long enough for him to notice.

"Sorry. It was my turn with the kid and her day-care lady was sick. I had to drive her to my mom's in Tikkurila. The ex wouldn't take her, said she had an important meeting, supposedly... what did the bosses say about that stolen body? It was in the headlines."

"We'll keep handling it for now. Check in with Arja and she'll give you the rundown. Conference room, 10:30."

The instant Oksanen shut the door behind him, my phone rang. I glanced at the number, but it didn't say anything to me.

"This is Kafka."

For a second, all I heard was vaguely agitated breathing.

"Did you get my letter?"

I snapped to attention. "Yes, thanks. I'm not sure I understood everything you were trying to say, and even less about why you needed Nevala's body."

"That was what she wanted. She said that would be her contribution to our struggle. I didn't want her to do that to herself, but God has granted us free agency. Which makes us almost like God. I honored Roosa's agency by using her, and before long I'll carry out her second wish, too."

"Is that the reason you stole her body a second time?"

"The one and only. You'll find out what I mean soon. Follow the signs of fire to their origins. You'll find a message for you there."

"Why don't you just give me the message now?"

"There's a time and a way to tell."

"At least tell me what battle you're talking about?"

"Against the dragon, against evil incarnate."

"Like Anteroinen, huh?"

"Yes. He was the first, but not the last. He was not able to escape God's wrath. Just as there are three goods, the Father, the Son, and the Holy Ghost, there are also three evils. Three is God's number, and evil mimics God in everything."

"In what way was Anteroinen evil?"

"You're a Jew, but I'm sure you're familiar with the New Testament. Jesus taught us to fear not those capable of killing the body but rather those who are able to destroy both body and soul. The worst thing you can do to a person is defile his soul and body. Don't worry, you'll find out everything in time."

"We know who you are. You know you'll be caught, so it would be wisest to turn yourself in – to me, say. We can talk things out —"

"I have responsibilities that I cannot leave unfulfilled."

"At least tell me what the Holy Vault means, then."

An impatient tone entered Laurén's voice. "The time hasn't come yet to reveal that."

While I still could, I quickly asked him, "Why did you want to tell all of this to me, specifically?"

"Isn't it clear, Ariel Kafka? Ariel means the light of God, the flame that will cleanse Jerusalem of her sins. You are the purifying flame, just as we are. Together we will burn the dragons so they can no longer wreak their evil on the souls of men."

The line went dead. I stared at my notebook, where I had only written five words: *follow the signs of fire.*

I went to see Stenman, but she wasn't in her office, and neither was Oksanen. I found Oksanen's absence particularly irritating. Knowing him, it had something to do with his cars. I went to have another word with Huovinen. At least *he* was there. I told him about the call and the information I had gathered immediately after.

"Did the number tell us anything?"

"Prepaid. Line was closed right after the call. I'll try to find out the IMEI code, but I'm guessing the phone was bought secondhand or under a false name."

"What Laurén told you about your name reveals the logic that's driving him. He's battling phantoms in his own head."

"I'm not sure about that."

Huovinen frowned.

"Even though he speaks in metaphors and is mixing everything up with his *Lord of the Rings* gibberish, the motive might be grounded in real events. And remember, he spoke in the plural. His exact words were: *you are the purifying flame, just as we are...* I believe the motive will become clearer once we find out if there was a connection between Anteroinen and Laurén. It's clear that Laurén wants publicity for the case and is prepared to put himself on the line to achieve it. I think he's the one who called *Ilta-Sanomat.*"

"I have to admit, I was pissed to see it in the paper on the way to work," Huovinen said. "I've already gotten three calls from reporters. Who knows, maybe the publicity will help us. But my instincts are still telling me this is going to end up a shitstorm for the department. If it turns out that Laurén is behind both deaths and has been evading us for years, we'll spend all spring pulling knives out of our backs."

"It'll be even worse if it turns out he warned us and was still able to kill someone else without us stopping him."

Huovinen's face darkened in concern. "This is starting to smell like a case for the National Bureau of Investigation. They already have their hands full, so I wouldn't bet they'll be clamoring to take it off our hands. But we should follow protocol and let them know what's going on. You're involved for the simple reason that Laurén specifically wanted you to investigate."

The further along I got in my story, the more worried Hyppönen, the CEO of the security company, looked. By the end, he looked almost hopeless. He loosened his tie; he seemed to be having a hard time breathing. The suspenders I caught a glimpse of under his jacket also seemed to tighten.

"I'm personally familiar with all our sites, including this one. Some outsider has to be involved, or else the intruder has gotten his hands on a badge belonging to one of the staff or the authorities. I'll get on it right away." Hyppönen jabbed briefly at his computer's keyboard with his sausage fingers, but he clearly wasn't comfortable with the machine. "This isn't exactly my forte... I'll bring in an expert." He shifted over to jabbing at the phone. "Seppo! Could you come to my office now... When I say now, I mean now!" he growled.

The expert, who based on his name tag and appearance was Hyppönen's son or otherwise of close genetic makeup, was there within ten seconds. He was carrying a laptop.

"The medical examiner's office... This detective here needs information on break-ins that occurred at the premises last night and the night before. The same corpse was taken from there twice."

"Are you serious —"

Hyppönen Sr.'s agitation was immediate. "I'm pretty sure the detective didn't come here to feed us a line. You just have a look with that computer of yours."

Hyppönen Jr. attacked his computer. His typing was so smooth that the bossman's anger melted. "Kids these days have such a different touch when it comes to gadgets. Computers are the future."

His sentiment would have been relevant thirty years ago, but better late than never.

"Our guy went there on both nights to close an external door that had been left open. The first visit took place at 2:42 a.m., and the second one the next evening at 10:17 p.m."

"What do you mean, open?" I asked.

"The alarm system notifies us if a door is left open for longer than ten minutes after office hours. When that happens, we drive to the site to check if the door is locked or if there's a technical malfunction in the alarm system… the second time it doesn't look like we even made it there, because the door closed before anyone headed out… the notification indicated there was no cause for concern. Could be that a janitor, police officer, funeral home, or someone else just left the door open by accident. It happens. One time an absentminded driver from the funeral home left the door open and the body in the loading zone. Some drunk kids rolled the stretcher up to the parking lot."

Hyppönen Senior wasn't amused by Junior's attempt to lighten the mood.

"I'm guessing the surveillance camera footage will show who removed the body?"

"Sure. It's on a hard drive in the control room —"

"The detective wants to see it, obviously," Hyppönen Sr. snapped.

The guy in the screen-filled control room was drinking coffee from a paper cup. When he saw Hyppönen Sr., he jumped and threw the cup into the trash so fast that some splashed out on him. Hyppönen Sr. didn't comment on this evident infraction.

Hyppönen Jr. referred to the note he'd made himself and browsed through the footage until he reached the right spot. "There it is."

We both bent down to look. A light-colored van parked in the loading ramp. Two men in hooded coveralls climbed out of the vehicle and walked right inside. A moment later they came back out, pushing a stretcher. The body was in the back of the van within seconds. Then they pushed the stretcher back inside, shut the door, and drove off. I wrote down the license-plate number.

"And the second time…" Hyppönen Jr. muttered as he fast-forwarded through the footage.

The second instance was a repeat of the first. It was even the same van.

"So the door was left unlocked on both occasions?"

"That's what it looks like… or it was… pretty sure," Hyppönen Jr. stammered.

"Was it or wasn't it?" Hyppönen Sr. insisted.

"It's also possible there was a technical malfunction —"

"How would a technical malfunction happen twice in a row right when the robbers happened to be there?" Hyppönen Sr. barked.

"I'm just saying —"

"Do you know who was on the premises when the thefts occurred?"

"Of course. Every badge leaves a record of every entrance or exit. When the door closed on the first evening or night the only person there was… medical examiner Vuorio, and on the second… forensic chemist Aili Jenssen, plus Vuorio again…"

5

I actually enjoyed pulling on-call shifts as lead investigator. Just about anything could turn up. If I couldn't sleep or wanted to get a taste of fieldwork, I was even known to join patrols for mundane responses. I called the duty desk a little before 1 a.m., just after they'd been notified of a man's body that had turned up in Kalasatama harbor. Oksanen was on call, too, and I headed over with him in his car. Its tortured engine set the silent streets roaring.

Two patrol cars were on the scene; the body had already been dragged out of the water. The guy who found it lived on a boat docked at the marina and was waiting for us in the back of one of the police vehicles. After coming home from a night out on the town and climbing aboard his vessel, the beam from his flashlight had struck the corpse, which was floating right next to his boat. It was a simple case. A wallet and driver's license were in the deceased's pocket. Based on them, we were able to identify him as a roadworthiness tester who'd been reported missing a couple of weeks earlier. There were no signs of violence. He lived in Hermanni and had disappeared on his way home. A buddy had dropped him off on the harbor road before continuing east in the cab they had shared. Presumably he'd stepped too close to the shore in the darkness and tumbled into the water. The embankment was steep and it was hard to climb out, especially with elevated blood-alcohol levels. In a city the size of Helsinki, there were enough sad fates for every day of the year.

"You want me to drop you at home or you wanna hit the hot dog stand at Karhupuisto?" Oksanen asked. "Come on, what do you say?"

I saw he could already taste a meat pie loaded with two sausages and all the trimmings. Because I'm not a cruel man, I agreed.

I'd lived in Kallio for almost a year during my time at the police academy. We passed my former student digs, on the fourth floor at the corner of Torkkelinkatu. I rewound through all the women I'd managed to lure to the place; I remembered six. They had all vanished from my life, but not without leaving behind their individual traces. One was a bank teller with a hysterical bent whom I'd dated a few times and even made the mistake of giving a key to my apartment. One night when I got home from a drinking binge with my classmates she was waiting for me and made a huge scene. She threw almost every article of clothing I owned out the window. Luckily my apartment faced the courtyard; my second-best sport coat got caught on the third-floor overhang and dangled there until I was able to retrieve it the next day. That wasn't so serious, but then she chucked out half the vinyl I'd collected. There went my Bellamy Brothers, Harry

Chapins, Jacques Brels, Nilssons, Nina Simones, and a whole bunch of other classics.

According to the car's temperature gauge, it was only a couple of degrees above freezing outside; the street glistened icily. The early spring night had an utterly unique feel. Summer wasn't right around the corner, but winter had been whipped. Nothing beat the romance of a drizzly spring night in Helsinki. It was one of the many things residents of warmer countries missed out on.

The hot dog stand was at the corner of Agricolankatu. We lined up to place our orders and went back to the car to eat them.

"One of the few joys of the night shift," Oksanen said, mouth full of sausage hash. He gulped down his food and confessed in a wistful tone: "When my ex and I used to live in Töölö, sometimes I'd go by during night shifts to screw. Now that pleasure is long gone."

Oksanen was divorced and, in typical Finnish fashion, argued with his ex over visitation rights. He twisted the radio knob to find a station he liked. The crooner Kari Tapio was bemoaning his fate. Oksanen joined in the chorus.

The crackle of the police radio prompted him to turn down the music. Dispatch announced that there was a fire in the woods near the postal distribution center at Ilmala; apparently at least one dead.

"Let's go check it out, since we're already on the road," I said.

I had to admit: Oksanen knew the city. Apparently there wasn't a side street or alley in Helsinki he hadn't raced down in one of his hot rods after getting his license.

He flipped a U-turn, turned left on Fleminginkatu, crossed Helsinginkatu and curved onto Aleksis Kiven katu, then right onto Sturenkatu and soon left again on Mäkelänkatu. After a few kilometers of racing, we arrived at Koskelantie, which before long turned into Hakamäentie.

Oksanen asked for instructions en route: "Calling about the burnt body at Ilmala. Give me a more precise location; I'm on Hakamäentie."

"Keep driving down Hakamäentie and turn north on Postintaival."

"Wait a sec," Oksanen said, because we had just arrived at the intersection. He dipped right. "Go ahead. I'm on Postintaival now."

"Continue north until you come to Metsäläntie. Turn left, and almost a kilometer later, left again, onto the little road leading into the woods."

"Roger."

The dirt road was so inconspicuous we almost drove past in the dark. As soon as we turned, I smelled the reek of smoke, and it wasn't long before I saw flashing blue and yellow lights. The road was so narrow, branches raked the sides of the car. Then Oksanen's lowered Audi bottomed out on a rock. He swore but kept driving, this time more slowly. Searchlights swept across the forest, which closed in more and more brazenly, twigs angrily slapping the Audi's sides. When a patrol car appeared in front of us, Oksanen pulled off to the side.

At first it looked as if a traveling circus had been erected in the middle of the secluded clearing. People were bustling about in the glow of the flashing lights. When I stepped out of Oksanen's car, I was assaulted by the pungent smell of smoke. The fire had been lit in the center of a small glade, and the pile of logs and branches was still smoldering. I had no trouble picturing the flames illuminating the treetops like an ancient sacrificial fire just twenty minutes earlier.

The fire chief on duty had already taken off his helmet. He walked up to me: "PD, I assume?"

"Yup. Dispatch said there's at least one body here."

"There's one."

"Where?" I asked. I'd been expecting a forest shack, or some dilapidated shed.

"There," the fire chief said, pointing at the smoking embers.

I stepped closer and pointed my flashlight at the charred wood. It took a moment to make out the foot sticking out from the logs, blackened with heat and smoke. Small and delicate, it had to belong to a woman, or a child.

"Someone's been taking inspiration from Indian funeral pyres," the fire chief said.

I moved closer, taking care not to leave any prints. My caution was unnecessary; the water from the hoses had transformed the vicinity into an enormous mud puddle. I circled the entire bonfire before I spied the right arm, the bone exposed by the flames. The rest of the body had burned to a crisp and was trapped in the smoldering wood.

"Who called it in?"

"One of the postal workers working the night shift, who took a shortcut on his way home. He lives in Pohjois-Haaga. He's sitting up there in the lead car, the Land Rover. This place is surrounded by hundreds of feet of dense forest. The flames weren't visible from any direction. We're guessing the fire had been burning for at least half an hour before we got here. We came from Haaga, so it only took us a few minutes."

I studied the structure of the fire. It had been constructed of crisscrossing logs, branches, and boards.

"Where did he get the firewood?" I mused out loud.

"Probably brought it in by car, same as the body. Most of that is sawn birch; the logs are over three feet long. You don't find that lying around. That means he needed at least a van. Gasoline was used as fuel." The fire chief shook his head. "I've seen plenty in my day, but I've never come across anything like this."

Oksanen walked up to me. "The tech team will be here in a minute."

"I guess our work here is done," the fire chief said. Then he appeared to remember something, and pulled an envelope out of his overall pocket. "Since you guys are with the PD, you probably know where to find this guy."

I took the envelope and glanced at it. A name had been printed on it: *Detective Ariel Kafka.*

"It was left on a stone a few meters from the burn. There was a little rock on top so it wouldn't blow away. You guys know this detective?"

I nodded. "Believe so."

"Well, then you can probably deliver it to the right man. Good luck with your investigation."

Oksanen sidled up to me and peered over my shoulder. "More fan mail? Take a look and see if it's from the same guy."

I went back to my car and turned on the overhead lights. I carefully slit open the envelope with gloved hands and pulled out the letter. Oksanen sat down next to me.

"The suspense is mounting," he muttered.

Detective Ariel Kafka

This letter was written so the police don't squander scarce resources on hunting down a nonexistent murderer. The body that rose to the heavens in the form of smoke is the same one you found yesterday in the apartment in Töölö. The immolation was her wish, which I promised to carry out, and did.

She was a good woman who deserved a beautiful send-off. A pure soul rises from the flames to return to the bosom of the Lord. An evil soul gets a foretaste of the agonies of hell even as it burns.

I also promised something new. If I were you, my dear Ariel, I would find out what happened to a man named Lars Sandberg.

Respectfully,

The Adorner of the Sacred Vault

"What does it say?" Oksanen asked.

I told him that, according to the author, the body was the same one we found in the apartment.

Oksanen was stunned. "You're kidding. The same body was snatched twice?"

I watched the line of fire trucks make a leisurely departure. "Yup. The body was taken from the pathology lab again."

"What a nutcase. Why is he writing you these letters?"

"Maybe he likes me," I said. To get rid of Oksanen, I added, "Bring the eyewitness over."

I sat down on the cold rock to ponder the letter. It had to be Laurén's handiwork again. If stealing the body and using it as a notepad was the first move in the game, as Vuorio suspected, was burning it the second one? Or had Laurén just called the game off?

I reread the line: *An evil soul gets a foretaste of the agonies of hell even as it burns.* It made me think of Anteroinen, who was badly burned before he was drowned. And what did the tip-off about Lars Sandberg mean? A thorough search of his name might bring some clarity to that.

"No, this is just the beginning," I said out loud.

"What's just the beginning?" Oksanen asked, catching me off guard as he walked up with the witness.

"Never mind."

6

"What about Lars Sandberg? Who's he?" Huovinen asked, twirling a pen between his fingers.

"I looked him up in the database and asked Stenman to dig a little deeper. He's a retired CFO, was murdered in Kotka two years ago. That case was never solved, either. A fisherman found Sandberg's body drifting in the outer archipelago. The legs had been weighted down, but the rope had rotted or chafed free and the body had risen to the surface. The corpse had been in the water over six months, so it was in pretty bad shape. The autopsy indicated that Sandberg was alive when he got the heave-ho. The most interesting detail was that his wrists were bound with heavy chains. That was never shared with the public."

"Aside from it being unsolved, does anything else link it to the Kouvola case or to Laurén?"

"Not yet, but we're looking into it."

"If there is a link, why is Laurén so intent on getting himself mixed up in such a serious crime? That makes as little sense as everything else to this point. I guess there's some consistency there, at least... I wonder if Arja has anything else for us yet..."

I called Stenman on the spot, and she promised to come right over. I asked her to pick up Oksanen on the way.

Before three minutes were up, they had both appeared in Huovinen's office. Stenman took a seat and started rifling through her papers. Oksanen remained standing behind her.

"Sit," Huovinen ordered. I could see the coolness in his face. Oksanen grabbed a chair and sat down between us.

"Sandberg is from Pietarsaari," Stenman said. "Had a business degree. Worked in payroll at the Turku ship-yards, then at an insurance company and a bank for a long period, after which he became chief financial officer at the B. E. Kajasto Foundation, retired on a disability pension in 2006. Married but divorced. One child, a 25-year-old son who's studying economics in Toronto. The ex-wife teaches high-school religion. According to her, Sandberg spent a lot of time at his cabin and was involved in his church youth group. I got the impres-sion that he was a bit of a bore, not very social. Neither Laurén's or Anteroinen's names meant anything to the ex-wife."

"Was there a note?"

"No, nothing like that."

"Maybe we should call the Pope, have him send an exorcist over to solve this case," Oksanen muttered.

"I also found two of Anteroinen's former co-workers who say that Anteroinen didn't have much going on, especially toward the end, except boozing with the local tough guys, betting at the racetrack, and going to baseball games. In his younger days, he had been a union activist of sorts, even served as union rep at the company. One of the friends thought he was a closeted homosexual."

"Great," Oksanen huffed.

"I had another chat with Laurén's ex-wife about Anteroinen and Sandberg. She didn't remember the names either."

"What was the foundation called where Sandberg worked again?" Huovinen asked.

"The B. E. Kajasto Foundation. Bertil Erik Kajasto was the founder. A shipbuilder and timber baron from Kotka who funneled the bulk of his sizable fortune into the foundation. Died in 1981 in a car crash."

I said I'd never heard of a foundation by that name.

"It's relatively well off, has had holdings in real estate, land, stocks, etc. Sandberg worked as CFO for nineteen years."

Oksanen had been fidgeting for a while now. He clearly didn't find the case worth his time.

"If a working stiff can give his opinion, there's nothing here we need to be involved in. The guy's a nutcase. Typical of us to be running around like crazy the second the media does a story."

I stared at Oksanen almost as coldly as Huovinen. "We have every reason to suspect that Laurén may have committed two murders, or at least that he has critical information on them."

"Some yokel cops blabbed everything they should have kept to themselves at the local pub and now the entire town knows all the ins and outs of the case. That's all it takes."

Even Stenman was caught off guard by Oksanen's outburst. "So you're saying you believe Laurén has somehow gleaned the details of crimes that took place in two different towns and is now using them for his plans and doesn't really know anything about the crimes?"

"A dozen shrinks couldn't figure out what's going through the head of that lunatic."

"Two lunatics, you mean. At least two people are involved here," I reminded Oksanen. "What if Laurén kills someone and we haven't taken any steps to prevent that from happening?"

"If I were you, I'd give Laurén's photo to the press and use publicity to smoke him out. If his picture's in the papers, he won't have the balls to go around killing people. Best of all, someone'll report him. Why is he so jacked to have you investigate the case, anyway?"

I didn't want to say anything about Laurén's "Ariel, Flame of God" ravings, so I lied without batting an eye: "No idea, but I'm OK with it. Arja and I are going to pay Laurén's ex-wife a visit. I want you to get in touch with the lead investigator in the Sandberg case and talk to the detective who worked on the Anteroinen case again. It was weird how stingy he was with me, so just tell him we're looking for a connection between the homicides. The tiniest link might be crucial."

Oksanen seemed less than enthusiastic and didn't bother hiding it, but he had to follow orders. I had more stripes.

7

Stenman and I met at 9 a.m. outside the residence of the former Seija Laurén. She was using her maiden name again and was now Seija Haapala. She lived in one of the newer apartment buildings in Arabianranta. Her airy home had been decorated in an Indian vibe, dark wood furniture accented with colorful pillows, boxes, candles, and jars. Our hostess looked like an ex-groupie who had retained most of the looks such pursuits demanded. Her hair was dyed red. My instinctive assessment was almost right on the mark.

"We met in college, when Reka's band performed at a party we were throwing. I was studying design at the University of Art and Design at the time and Reka was study-ing music at the Sibelius Academy. We were both so artsy, so artsy. He came back to my dorm afterward and spent the night. The usual story. Our daughter Mandi was born three years later, but we got married before that. The first years were wonderful. He was so much fun when he was sober, but when he was drunk, the darker side started coming out more and more often. He should have stayed away from alcohol and pot. We might still be married if he had."

"We're interested in learning about his friends from childhood and adolescence."

"I already told you what I know. Was it you I talked to?" she asked, nodding in Stenman's direction.

"Yes. I asked you to spend some time thinking back while looking at old photographs, to see if they might help you remember something."

"I did, but it didn't spark anything. Why don't you guys just sit back and wait? Reka will come out of the woodwork when he needs help."

"We'd like to find him as soon as possible."

"Why? Are you afraid he'll do something to himself..." Seija raised a hand to her mouth. "Has he already done something to someone?"

"Not to our knowledge," I said.

"Two detectives wouldn't go to the trouble of calling and then coming by if it weren't something serious."

"We want to make sure nothing serious happens. What about his musician friends? Has he been in touch with them?"

The look of concern didn't fade from Seija's face.

"Two died from overdoses, one lives in Australia, and another one somewhere up in Lapland, in the sticks... all I know about him is his first name, Jukka, they called him Juki... did you know Reka was convicted of narcotics possession about ten years ago?"

"Your ex-husband ended up in psychiatric treatment during your time together. Why do you think that was?"

"Not because of me, that's for sure. Maybe it ran in the family. Reka said his mom was schizophrenic. Since the family was upper crust, it was kept secret as long as possible."

"Did something happen while you were together that triggered the illness?"

"I think it was the marijuana. When we divorced, Reka moved to Tibet for more than two years to seek enlightenment. He sure didn't find any there, came back darker than ever. If you have a family history of schizophrenia, smoking pot's a bad idea. I can tell you from experience that marijuana isn't the innocent natural product people say it is."

"Did you ever talk with the doctors who treated him?"

"They wouldn't say anything, even to me. Patient confidentiality, apparently. They wouldn't have told me if he'd confessed he planned on killing during his next visit home. OK, he didn't kill me. So I guess the treatment worked."

"What about the names I mentioned, Lars Sandberg and Leo Anteroinen?" Stenman asked.

"They still don't say anything. Who are they?"

"Anteroinen was born in 1951, comes from Kurikka, a custodian or maintenance man, moved to Kouvola at some point. Sandberg was born in Pietarsaari in 1953 and was a financial officer by profession. Worked at a bank, an insurance company, and the B.E. Kajasto Foundation in Kotka."

"They're both ten years older than Reka. He didn't hang out with anyone that old… why do you think he knew them?"

"We just want to find out if he did."

"You guys don't try to figure out stuff like that for no reason... what did the one guy do for a living, again?"

"CFO."

"The other one."

"Anteroinen was both a custodian and a maintenance man."

Haapala ruffled her red mane, clearly trying to access memories that had faded long ago. I reflected that she must have been really hot when she was younger. She was still beautiful and seemed to subconsciously give off lighter-than-air sex molecules. Arja probably didn't notice it, but I was having a hard time concentrating.

"Something crossed my mind, but I lost it. I think Reka talked about some custodian once in a negative tone. It somehow stuck with me, because he usually talked trash about the big shots and left the grunts alone."

"When was the last time he was in touch with you?" I asked.

Seija looked at me as if she were weighing something up. What was going through her head, I had no idea. I suppose I'd assessed her appearance, too. Maybe she'd sensed that.

"It's been months, I can't even remember exactly. Had to do with spending time with his daughter. We agreed that he'd call when he wanted to see Mandi. They usually met in town, went out to eat, the usual."

"Do you know, does he have a second home – a summer cabin or the like? He has to be living somewhere."

"Not that I know of... at one point he talked about buying an RV, but I don't know if he did."

I jotted down in my notebook: *RV?* It was the first note I had made.

"If your ex-husband hated something, do you know who or what that would be?" Stenman asked, shrewdly.

"Reka was an angry young man. At one point he hated everything, especially authority figures: politicians, police officers, rich people, teachers, deans, professors. The last of these was presumably because he was kicked out of the university, even though he loved music."

"Was he religious?"

"Was he ever, and probably still is, at least in his own way. That ran in the family, too. His dad was religious; that whole side of the family was. I think there were even a couple of pastors in there, or at least preachers. That was probably one of the reasons we broke up. When Reka was flying high, he wanted me to believe, too, and to get involved in that scene, but I wouldn't."

"What about when he was flying low?" I asked.

"Pure hell. He was constantly flitting between heaven and hell. When he was young, he planned on studying theology. I suppose he studied it at some level at the Daybreak Academy, too, but then music entered the picture, along with booze, weed, women, me…"

"The Daybreak Academy?"

Seija chuckled. "And the boarding house was called the Daybreak House. Pretty pious, huh? The Academy was run by the Church of the Redemption. Reka attended high school there. The couple of friends I mentioned were from that period. I heard one is a professor at Oxford these days. The other was a doctor but shot himself. I don't know either of their names. Reka never wanted to introduce me to his friends, and to be honest, I wasn't that interested in meeting them."

"One last question," I said. "Does the Sacred Vault say anything to you, or the Adorner of the Sacred Vault?"

"It sure does. The Sacred Vault was a secret society founded by the kids at the Daybreak Academy; Reka was one of the founding members. Try and guess if I got sick of hearing about Sacred Vault this, Sacred Vault that when he was drunk."

Stenman and I exchanged glances. Seija's revelation might prove a shortcut to the secret.

"What was the point of the secret society?"

"What's the point of any secret society boys join? I guess it satisfied some yearning for excitement and mysticism in a rigid environment. I think it kind of goes with the territory at that age, like building forts and mopeds. Now kids that age have computer games and Harry Potter."

"Your ex-husband must have told you something about this club, if he mentioned it frequently?" Stenman said.

"It had religious undertones, but there's nothing weird about that, either, when you consider that a lot of those boys came from religious families. One of their dads was a bishop, I think, and there were a few who were pastors' sons. It was all about some battle between good and evil; the boys from the Vault represented good, of course. They had their own persnickety rules and rituals they weren't allowed to talk about or they'd be denied God's goodness and truth for thirty years. The number symbolized the thirty pieces of silver given to Judas."

30 pieces of silver, I wrote in my notebook.

"So who represented evil, then?" I asked.

"The conversation never got any deeper than that, because when he saw I thought the whole thing was silly, he got mad and shut up like a clam."

"Apparently Reka held a high position in the society's ranking?"

"I guess. One time he showed me a picture of him posing in some ceremonial outfit. It was a white apron and a short cape with a hood. I laughed so hard I almost peed my pants. Reka was furious."

"Was there anyone else in the picture?"

"Three other members of the club. They were the only ones who had the right to break the seals that contained the Gospel of the Three Angels."

Seija laughed, but suddenly her laughter turned into gasping tears. "I shouldn't have laughed. It was a big deal to Reka. He thought of himself as some sort of champion of truth."

I rewound a little: "Going back to evil, did he ever even hint as to who represented evil to them?"

Seija took a moment to wipe her eyes. "According to Reka, they had one ceremony where they symbolically slayed evil. In it, evil was represented by a wolf in sheep's clothing. That's all I remember. I think evil was an abstraction for them, not real. What would boys that age know about genuine evil? They'd all lived sheltered lives."

Seija's cell phone rang on the hall table, and she hurried off to answer. Based on what we could hear, it was her daughter calling.

"Sorry. My daughter. Where were we...? I made it clear I thought the whole secret society business was childish. Reka was somehow stuck on it, even though it had been God knows how many years since high school."

"Do you have the photograph of the Vault members posing together?" Stenman asked.

"Are you kidding? Reka guarded it with his life; it was his only picture of the whole thing. Besides, like I said, everything was supposedly top secret."

"What about other pictures of your ex-husband?"

"Of course."

Seija started rummaging through the living-room cabinets and hoisted a thick brown photo album onto the table.

"Here are a few of the most recent ones." The photos were loose between the pages, and Seija handed them to Stenman. I'd seen the twenty-year-old picture of Laurén we had requisitioned from the driver's licensing office. These photographs, on the other hand, showed a narrow-faced forty-year-old gazing somewhere over the photographer's left shoulder. He had an absentminded stare on his face, as if pondering some personal problem that demanded rapid resolution. He looked like he hadn't been getting much sleep. The stubble, greasy dark hair, and red plaid flannel shirt gave a disheveled impression.

"We'll borrow these," I said.

"Feel free. They were taken about three years ago. He helped out when Mandi and I moved here."

"Can I have a look at the album?"

Seija hesitated, but then handed it to me. Stenman came and stood next to me so we would be seeing the same thing.

The photos were the typical shots taken of a budding relationship. First came kisses and caresses, then a little more distance. Pictures from Linnanmäki theme park, Jim Morrison's grave, the Eiffel Tower, parties, a summer cabin – apparently the in-laws'. A few shots of the band, with Laurén playing solos. A group of people standing around an old-fashioned Lucifer grill, grilling sausages. In the background, berry bushes and apple trees and a cute white cottage with green trim. Judging by the size of the apples, it was already August. Then the daughter, Mandi, appeared in the young couple's life and grew in leaps and bounds. Mandi at the maternity clinic, Mandi crawling on the lawn, Mandi in her kindergarten nativity play, Mandi at the beach somewhere in southern Europe, Mandi at Särkänniemi amusement park, and, before long, we were already at Mandi's first day at school.

"The dad and daughter seem to have a close relationship," I offered.

"Two peas in a pod."

"Could we have your daughter's phone number?"

"She's a minor," Seija immediately said.

"She's not suspected of anything. Maybe she'll remember something her dad told her that could help us."

"I'd feel better about it if I knew why it is you need our help."

As investigative lead, communicating about the case was my call. I was also free to discuss the investigation if necessary. I decided to avail myself of my right and crack the veil of secrecy.

"Your husband contacted us, and the conversation left us with the impression that he intends on committing a violent crime. If that's the case, we want to prevent it, so he doesn't get himself into deep trouble."

Seija didn't appear to take this information very seriously. "Who was he threatening, supposedly? Reka isn't violent; at most he talks tough. When he used to get mad at me, he'd slam the door and disappear for a few hours. He never displayed any violent tendencies. I was more violent with him. I threw a glass at him once, and another time I broke the skin at the corner of his eye with a wooden hanger. But he never responded violently."

"He suffers from schizophrenia," I reminded her.

"He did back then, too."

"We don't want to leave anything to chance. It's for his own good, too. Can we get Mandi's number?" Stenman asked again.

Seija wrote the number down on the corner of the newspaper, tore it off, and handed it to Stenman.

"One more question. According to the information we have, your ex-husband was dating. The woman's name was Roosa Nevala. Did you ever meet her, or did he tell you anything about her?"

"No. Sometimes he hinted that he had no shortage of women. He might have even been telling the truth. He knew how to get women to like him if he wanted to."

"What do you think?" I asked Stenman as we stepped into the elevator. At the same time, I pulled out my phone and saw Huovinen had called three times and texted me: *Call ASAP!* The message had arrived fifteen minutes ago.

"Did you notice what —" Stenman began.

"Wait a sec. Huovinen."

I brought up Huovinen's number. "Sorry I couldn't call. We were talking to Laurén's ex-wife and my phone was on silent."

Huovinen ignored my apology. "Have you seen today's *Ilta-Sanomat?*"

"No. What's in it?"

"That funeral pyre in Metsälä the night before last. They were on the scene, filming, when that lunatic lit it. It's also online. There's a limit, even with the tabloids. I think we're talking about criminal incitement."

"Who wrote the article?"

"That same reporter who went public with the theft of the body, Maisio or Moisio or whatever. For some reason, Laurén has taken the guy into his confidence. Could you talk to him again? I'll have a word with the editor-in-chief."

Huovinen and I agreed that I would come see him the minute I got back to the office.

"What now?" Stenman asked.

I related what Huovinen had told me. "There's a reporter who hasn't spent a lot of time considering what it's going to feel like for that woman's loved ones to see her body go up in flames. You were saying something before I called Huovinen."

"Laurén's wife claimed his fellow band members were either dead or have been out of the picture for years. That's not true."

"What do you mean?"

"Did you see the shot of the band called Holy Night?"

"What about it?"

"The other guitarist was Ola Sotamaa. He's a regular presence on television, one of the music shows. He's some sort of music journalist."

8

I was getting the sense that the case was gradually opening up. Information was accumulating. One good clue could produce a rich harvest, lead down many new paths. The worst was treading water, blind.

I looked at Oksanen, who was staring at his notebook. Stenman was sipping tea from a fire-engine-red mug.

"Didn't get much, just like I figured," Oksanen began. "The lead investigator on the Sandberg case hadn't ever heard of Anteroinen or Laurén. I asked about possible motives, but according to him they never came up with one. Sandberg wasn't some shady character; he was an upstanding citizen. He lived by himself in his seaside house and didn't have any beef with anyone. Neighbors spoke well of him. Didn't host rowdy barbecues or play his stereo too loud, didn't test his Black & Decker in the middle of the night, didn't own a leaf blower, and observed Sunday silence. They eventually arrived at the conclusion that it was a random act of violence. He'd told a neighbor that he was headed out to the skerry to go jig-fishing for perch. According to the neighbor, he used to spend a lot of time fishing alone. The boat was discovered where it was supposed to be, the man four kilometers away in the water. They never found any eye-witnesses to what happened."

I expressed disbelief at the randomness theory. "He was abducted, bound, driven a few miles in a boat, and thrown alive into the sea with weights on. Someone went to a lot of trouble. Plus there's the connection to the Anteroinen case. He was thrown into the septic tank alive, too."

"Either way, random victim is where the local investi-gators ended up."

"What about the investigator in the Anteroinen case?"

"Didn't seem to care for my Helsinki accent... Claimed he told you everything he knew and then some," Oksanen said.

"That's all you have?"

"I did some more checking of my own. I found out one pretty interesting thing about that foundation. It went to court with the founder's only son over the money. And for good reason, too. There was almost thirty million in cash alone. This was back in the markka days, of course. The son was paid a few hundred thousand for his pain and suffering. Works as a fireman these days. He's out of town. I left him a message and told him to call."

"Where did you come by this information?"

"A reporter I know at the *Helsingin Sanomat* found an article on him in the archives. It was Sandberg who handled the estate on behalf of the foundation."

I was disappointed in the material Oksanen had gath-ered. "So you didn't find any links between the cases?"

"No, but Anteroinen's former co-worker said Anteroinen had worked somewhere in Häme for a few years in the late '70s and that he'd run into some sort of trouble out there. According to his colleague, they were supposed to go on a company trip to Hämeenlinna to tour some other company, but Anteroinen refused. Said he hated the place, had bad memories of it, but wouldn't say what."

"Worked where?"

"The colleague didn't know. Apparently as custodian or maintenance man, though, just like everywhere else."

"Were any of the employers listed in Anteroinen's pension records in Häme?" I asked Stenman.

"Not that I recall, no."

"What was the name of that academy where Laurén went to boarding school?"

"The Daybreak Academy," Stenman said. I googled it.

The website for the Church of the Redemption appeared at the top of the list of results. I went to the site and clicked Contact.

"It's near Forssa," Stenman said.

"Call Daybreak and check if Anteroinen worked there as a custodian in the 1970s," I ordered Oksanen.

"Now?"

"Now. And then come straight back here. I need to talk to you." I was unable to filter the annoyance out of my voice.

Oksanen left the room.

Stenman sensed my irritation and didn't say anything. I continued as if nothing had happened: "So at least we know that the Sacred Vault really existed and wasn't just some delusion of Laurén's. Seeing as how he's dragged it into his crusade for vengeance, I'm thinking we'll find the motive in the same place as the Sacred Vault."

"You mean we'll find the motive at Daybreak?"

"Maybe 'place' is the wrong word, so not necessarily at Daybreak. It might also be the time period, events that took place then. Set up a meeting with Sotamaa. You'd think a bandmate would be close enough you'd tell him stuff you wouldn't tell other people. Bands drink, smoke pot, and talk shit, at least when they're on tour."

Stenman rose to leave.

"And feel free to offer any good suggestions."

I tried to call Laurén's number, but it was still out of service. A stack of papers waiting to be reviewed stood on my desk, but I was having a hard time concentrating. It was a little after eleven, and at one o'clock a case I'd been lead on and that had made the front page of the papers would be tried in the Helsinki Court of Appeal. The defendant was a woman who had taken out a hit on her husband and hired an Estonian hitman. The guy had carried out the commission, which we found evidence of when he turned up in Tarto.

Oksanen rushed in just as I was checking the time the trial would start. "Nada. I told you. This is a waste of time; it's not like we don't have plenty of real work to be doing."

"What's a waste of time?"

"No one by the name of Leo Anteroinen worked for the Church of the Redemption in the 1970s or any other point. The administrative assistant started working there in 1978."

"Good thing we checked."

"Is there anything else?"

"As a matter of fact, there is. Sit."

I pulled out a copy of Saimi Vartiainen's letter from my drawer and passed it across the desk to Oksanen.

He accepted it, looking a little perplexed. The further he read, the darker his face grew.

"This is bullshit," he snapped, flinging the letter down on my desk. "I know this old trout. For some reason she's always been a bitch to me."

"So you've had dealings with the company?"

"A few times, as representative of the rally club. The owner, Berg, is a nice guy who's into motorsports. That's how I know him. It's completely natural for me to drop in and say hi when I'm there getting stuff for the club. It would be rude not to."

"So you haven't received the perks Vartiainen mentions?"

"What constitutes a perk? The club is a big customer. Of course we get parts and supplies for a better price than some jerk off the street. Besides, Berg told me he'd be happy to do a little sponsoring. In return, his company's logo appears in the club paper and on our cars. There's nothing weird about that. What would be weird would be us being put in a worse position than everyone else because of our profession —"

"The profession of police officer is not just any profession. Taking them to the cleaners for thousands of euros' worth of perks —"

"If I were you, as a kike, I wouldn't talk about taking anyone to the cleaners and —" Oksanen realized what he'd said and stopped as if he'd hit a brick wall. "If you have any questions, check with Commissioner Kalliola at the ministry. He knows everything about the sponsorship arrangement and the club's purchases. They were approved by him, every single one."

"As a kike, I'm asking you directly, because I'm your direct superior. I received the letter from Huovinen and he ordered me to do some preliminary checking into the matter."

"That bargain-basement male model. I've said everything I have to say." Oksanen left brusquely.

I looked at my screensaver, but didn't see it. There was as much prejudice and anti-Semitism on the force as there was among the public at large, maybe more. The profession was one of a kind when it came to feeding prejudices. Still, none of my co-workers had ever called me a kike before, not even during the final beer-soused moments of a long night together at the sauna.

The profession hardened you, and I'd always thought of myself as thick-skinned, callused. Still, it felt like I had just been slapped across the face. It stung, and it pissed me off, all at the same time.

9

Looking around at the editorial room at *Ilta-Sanomat*, I was reminded of the old saying: those who live in glass houses shouldn't throw stones. Apparently crime reporter Jyri Moisio had never heard of it. He was chucking rocks like there was no tomorrow.

"Let's go into the conference room. The editor-in-chief will join us in a minute."

Moisio was big and had an unforthcoming air about him. His short hair was gelled straight up. Somewhere between the range of thirty and forty. I caught a glimpse of a showy Rolex peeking out from under his Gant sweater. It definitely hadn't been bought from a street vendor in Thailand.

I had no trouble interpreting the reporter's body language. It spoke of reluctance. Translated into words, the message would have been: go ahead and say what you're going to say, but don't think for a minute it's going to make a lick of difference.

Through the glass partition wall, I saw a man with the demeanor of an editor-in-chief approach, along with the familiar briefcase-wielding suit. The editor-in-chief's belt was cinched so tightly that his constricted stomach flesh bulged over it.

"You don't mind, do you? I asked our legal counsel, Markku Pyysalo, to join us. Perhaps you know each other?"

I had run into Pyysalo at the courthouse, but I couldn't claim to know him. He generally handled white-collar clients, criminal cases less frequently.

"We've met," Pyysalo said. "And I also know your brother Eli through work. We even have some clients in common. I have a lot of respect for your brother."

The editor-in-chief felt like it was his responsibility to open up the meeting. "Of course I know what brings you here, Ariel – if I may call you Ariel – but Pyysalo and I just reviewed the case from top to bottom, and we couldn't find any legal issues.

"The only possible fit is criminal incitement, or else the provocation clause, but that's not relevant here. Our reporter headed to the scene after receiving a tip, which falls under the rubric of completely normal journalistic practices. He didn't know what he would find there, and he had no opportunity to prevent the incident."

"There's been a misunderstanding. Who said we were accusing you of having committed any crimes?"

The editor-in-chief and Pyysalo exchanged glances.

I felt some glee at having successfully surprised them. Threatening a reporter would have been stupid. That would just further distort their notion of their own importance.

"Then why are we here?" Pyysalo asked.

"We're proposing cooperation so we can find the individual who stole the body and burned it. Cooperation that will also benefit you."

"How?"

"If you help us, we can agree that you'll be the first to get any information on the investigation."

"In addition to our responsibility to protect our sources, we're also bound by confidentiality," the editor-in-chief reminded me, trying to look as if it meant anything to him.

"We call that bound to secrecy, so we're even."

"What could we do to help the police?"

"By telling us what you know about the perpetrator, why he contacted your reporter specifically – and twice, for that matter. That indicates that he might contact you in the future as well."

"He told me he liked one of my articles," Moisio said.

"Which one?"

"It was on the malfeasance of the CEO of a state-owned company. He felt I had gathered a lot of important information and hadn't softened the story."

"I suppose you asked why he wanted publicity?"

"Wait, we haven't reached an agreement yet," Pyysalo jumped in, before Moisio could answer.

"I told you what we want and what you'll get. What's not clear?"

"Go on," the editor-in-chief said.

"He said this was about a much bigger matter and he wanted a good reporter to follow the story from the start and do a proper write-up on it. He didn't go into any further detail."

"Did he identify himself?"

Moisio glanced at Pyysalo and the editor-in-chief.

"He didn't tell us, but we also know how to acquire information," the editor-in-chief said on his reporter's behalf. "And I'll answer your next question while I'm at it. We don't have his phone number. You mind if I ask some questions, too? The VCU doesn't investigate the theft of bodies. Why are you guys handling the case?"

I told the truth: "It was my bad luck to be on duty when the case came up, and I got stuck with it for the meantime. As far as I'm aware, there's no unit dedicated to handling cases like this."

"You also happened to be there when the body was burned."

"How do you know?"

"We hung back around at the fringes to see how things would unfold," the reporter said. "Why did he leave a letter addressed specifically to you?"

"I wish I knew. Maybe he saw my name in the paper."

"My hunch is he handpicked Moisio from the press and you from the police force. For some reason, he trusts you two," the editor-in-chief said. "We're prepared to cooperate on that basis, but it has to be advantageous to us, too. Of course, we're always happy to help the police in any way we can."

Moisio seemed to grow gloomier. "As a journalist, I have to protect my sources. I can't betray his trust, no matter what the police promise us. The police do their job; we do ours. If it starts getting around that we're leaking information to the police, no one will ever dare contact us again."

"It would be important for us to know immediately next time he contacts you."

The reporter clearly disapproved. "You want me to set a trap for him?"

"Surely your job description doesn't include helping those suspected of crimes avoid arrest."

"Of course we'll have to weigh cooperation case by case, but in principle we're prepared to cooperate, and understand our responsibility," the editor-in-chief said.

I spent another fifteen minutes in the editorial offices, but we didn't get much further. Stenman was waiting for me in a car outside. We'd be going to our next meeting together.

10

Sotamaa had all the hallmarks of an old rocker: the jeans, the leather jacket, the mullet, and the sideburns. He had suggested we meet at the bar at the Hotel Pasila. The public radio building and police HQ were both a stone's throw from there, so that worked for us. I brought Stenman along.

He glared at me accusingly. "What did Reka do now? Caught for possession? Leave the poor guy alone, for God's sake."

A glass of orange juice stood on the table in front of Sotamaa. A beer would have been more fitting.

"Not this time. We're actually looking for two of his old acquaintances, and believe you can help us."

"Why don't you just ask him?"

"We haven't been able to reach him," Stenman said. "When did you two last see each other?"

"It's been at least six months. How did you find out about me?"

"His wife," I said, then corrected myself: "Ex-wife."

"Hmm. I have fifteen minutes before we start taping. Shoot."

"When did you and Laurén get to know each other?"

"As students. First at boarding school, then we started studying music here in Helsinki at the same time."

"You guys were also in the same band."

"True, but that only lasted about a year. In college we played at parties for free food and booze. He met his future wife at one of them. He was already so unstable back then I knew the relationship would crash and burn. Seija, the future wife, studied at UIAH. She didn't dig us too much, said we were a bad influence on Reka. I wasn't at the wedding; I don't think I was even invited. As I recall, they got hitched at the magistrate's office."

"Unstable in what way?" I asked.

"We all smoked pot, but it didn't really suit Reka. He'd shoot right off into outer space. He thought he was God's chosen one, destined to suffer like Jesus, but he wouldn't turn the other cheek and would destroy evil for good."

"What did he mean by evil?"

"Money, for one. He thought it was the bait the Devil used to lure the weak into traps. So anything involving money was to be avoided. As far as I know, he was from a wealthy family, so maybe it was a projection of a bad conscience, or rebelling against your father, take your pick. Back then if you were socially conscious you were leftist. He came up with some theses of his own, like Martin Luther back in the day. Reka battled his own demons like Luther, but he wasn't satisfied using a bottle of ink as his weapon. I got an ominous vibe from it sometimes. I'm a peaceful man. Tail end of the peace and love generation."

Stenman continued in this vein: "Did this evil take human form? I mean, were there any real people he considered evil?"

"He didn't like cops, for one, or politicians. But that's pretty normal," Sotamaa chuckled. "If you ask me, the contradiction was that he talked a lot without saying much. He'd tease you but never go all the way, as they say. I didn't get how he could be so gung-ho and so constantly mysterious at the same time."

"We're mostly looking for two people. One is named Leo Anteroinen, the other is Lars Sandberg."

Sotamaa shook his head. "The names don't say anything. Who are they?"

"Laurén's childhood friends."

"The Sacred Vault gang, huh?"

"So you've heard of it?"

"More than I wanted to. That's actually what I was talking about when I said that he talked a lot but was still mysterious. Reka would go on and on about it when he was drunk or stoned, but he never got very specific. From what I could gather, it was some sort of secret society from his high-school days. I never did figure out what the point was. I was only at the Daybreak Academy a year and a half, and then my family moved to Helsinki. That's why I was never as up on it as he was."

"Do you know the names of any of the members?"

"Nope. That was top secret, too. If you told, you'd be banished from the Vault for thirty years. A horrible punishment, I'm sure. All I know is that one of the members is a big cheese at Nokia nowadays and another one's a professor in England. I haven't even met any —"

"But you still attended the same school for over a year. What do you know about Reijo's time at boarding school?"

"Not much. I know he didn't dig it. It was a boarding school; discipline was tough. I guess his old man made him go. Both his parents were religious. Small-town big shots. Pharmacists."

"He ended up in a psychiatric unit. What did he tell you about that?"

"Who would want to talk about that?"

"Do you know if Reka has any other friends besides you?"

"I wouldn't call myself a friend. We played together in a band, that's it. When he was sober he was a nice guy, smart and funny, but when he was drunk he'd sink in some seriously murky waters."

"Still."

"There was a woman. They met about a year ago. Reka called me from the lobby of the main broadcast building and asked if I had time to meet for coffee. I went, and she was with him. Reka seemed surprisingly normal, we reminisced about the past. She was pretty quiet, barely said two words the whole time."

"Do you remember her name?" Stenman asked.

"Isn't coming to mind."

"Could it be Roosa?"

"Could be. She was good-looking. Clearly younger than Reka. Red hair; I don't know if it was natural, but it looked like it. Reka's ex was a redhead, too —"

Stenman pulled out a photo of Roosa Nevala. "Was this the woman?"

Sotamaa glanced at the picture. "That's her."

"Didn't Reka tell you anything about her? Where they met, her profession, anything else?"

"No. Just introduced her, said this is my girlfriend, Roosa."

"Why did he come see you?"

Sotamaa plumbed his memory for a moment. "Now I remember. He asked if I could look up information on a few people in our news and personality archives. I told him the archives were for internal use only, but he wouldn't let it drop. Said that they were basically his old friends and the info wouldn't harm them."

"Who did he want information on?"

"One was a guy who did a dissertation on church music, if I'm remembering right. Can't think of the name, but there can't be too many of them. The other one I remember. He was a lawyer, name was Silén. I remember that because when I was in the army, there was a guy with the same name in my squad. And the third... what was your name again, sorry, I didn't really catch it..."

"Kafka."

"I guess I did after all. I thought I remembered wrong; it's a pretty weird coincidence. The third one was Ariel Kafka. I guess that's you."

"What kind of information did he want on me?"

"The kinds of cases your name had been mentioned with in the news. Of course, I asked Reka why he was interested in some detective, and he claimed he wanted to interview you for some book or novel he was writing. I didn't buy it. I haven't heard from him since."

"What kind of information did he want on Silén?"

"A story about some foundation's funding and money Silén had lost. There had been a segment on it on some current-affairs program ten, fifteen years ago. I found the script for the show and gave it to Reka. He said he'd get back to me about some other stories, but I told him sorry, I couldn't help him out anymore, because the archives are for internal use only."

"Laurén's interested in you for some reason. I wonder why?" Stenman pondered as we walked back to HQ. I couldn't help giving her the once-over. She was wearing jeans, a short suede jacket, and a Burberry scarf. Pricey brands on a police officer's salary, but she'd been married to a guy with money, no prenup. I'd heard Stenman had gotten half his net worth in the divorce. And held onto it, unlike the ex-husband, whose half had evaporated during a tax-administration investigation of invoice fraud.

I told her Laurén's explanation for why he had taken me into his confidence.

"The Flame of God. Can't say I get it."

"Me neither."

"The lawyer Sotamaa mentioned is most likely or definitely named Henry Silén. He's been missing for almost two months."

"How do you know?"

"I read the tabloids. His wife reported him missing. Suspects he's dead. But his co-workers think he skipped town and is living overseas, because he made a mess of his finances and those of some clients."

Now I remembered the headlines from a couple of months back, about the lawyer's mysterious disappearance.

"Find out who's investigating," I said.

"Strange coincidence, Laurén asking about Silén a little while before the guy vanishes. What if the same thing happened to Silén that happened to Sandberg? Dropped to the bottom of the sea."

"While you're at it, find out if there are any connections between Silén, Sandberg, Laurén, and Anteroinen." I made a silent wish that no connections would turn up. If they did, we might have a genuine serial killer on our hands.

"Where's Oksanen? I haven't seen him all day," Stenman said.

"Out sick."

Oksanen had sent a text message that morning informing me that the doctor had given him two weeks of sick leave because of degenerative back trouble.

"Flu?"

A nasty fever had been going around the department. Arja and I were two of the few not to catch it.

"Nah, it was something else."

Stenman glanced at me almost as if she suspected something. Woman's intuition. "Did something happen?"

Superiors were forbidden from talking about their subordinates' affairs with other subordinates. So I settled for a lie. "No."

The look on Stenman's face said she didn't believe me.

11

The bureaucrats at the Ministry of the Interior could be grouped, roughly speaking, into two categories: ascetics who ran marathons, rowed in competitions, cycled to work from March to November, and ate nothing but supplements intended for that purpose and special fiber-rich cereals that set the digestion working. Then there was the softer species that had a taste for the good life. In the minds of this class, the inherent advantages of their station – whether opera tickets sent by advertising agencies, Estonian wild-boar hunts sponsored by banks, or cooking courses billed to insurance companies – were meant to be enjoyed. Anywhere they went, there was at least one acquaintance in proximity who was packing a company credit card. Arto Kalliola belonged to the latter caste. I amused myself by imagining his bulging gut in a pair of tight rally coveralls.

We met for coffee at Market Square, in a tent that looked like a ramshackle shelter for construction workers. The chill in the air was banished by patio heaters. Aside from us, only a few tourists were present.

Kalliola sipped at his coffee, then lowered his cup to the table and focused on me. "Pleasure meeting you. I've heard a lot of good things about you… you fish?"

I detected a Turku accent.

"No, except for the odd angling at my brother's cabin."

"We're setting up a trout-fishing trip to Ahvenanmaa this spring with a great bunch of guys. There's still room to join if —"

I encouraged Kalliola to get to the point. "I get seasick easily. You wanted to talk?"

"Super you could meet on such short notice; I figured it would be best to talk face to face. Professional to professional. As I mentioned, Oksanen called and told me about the allegations contained in the letter you received at the department."

The way Kalliola pronounced the word "allegations" told me there was no mistaking his views on the matter. Old-time crooks spoke of snitches with the same disdain. "I have to say, I'm speechless. It's extremely unfortunate that such a beneficial and worthwhile hobby has been besmirched with such unpleasant accusations. It's incalculable, the amount of positive PR the Finnish police enjoys thanks to the activities of its rally club. We've gotten to know our brothers and sisters in blue from countless other countries, up to the highest echelons. I can vouch that every minute devoted to it has been more than worth the investment."

I didn't respond. The tourists had left, leaving us the sole customers in the tent. Our only companion was the salesperson reading the paper behind the counter.

"I understand, of course, that the department is between a rock and a hard place."

The only one between a rock and a hard place was Kalliola, which is why I said: "I don't see it that way."

I saw Kalliola's brow furrow. The guy's forehead was more expressive than the average Finn.

"What do you mean? I spoke with your superior, Superintendent Huovinen, and at least he indicated he felt badly about the situation you've been placed in."

Out of sheer politeness, I thought, but I said: "I mean we're taking the steps the circumstances require. The ministry has drafted precise instructions for situations like these. And we're following them."

Kalliola's round face turned toward the two Russian women peering in through the door flap. They were wearing furs and tall, shiny leather boots. They turned away.

"Ladies of the night out and about during the day," Kalliola enthused. "An old pro can always spot them…" Kalliola realized he had wandered off topic, and in the wrong direction to boot. "And what do the circumstances require, in your view?"

"We'll be interviewing the individual who sent the letter, of course, as well as the company's owner. After that, we'll ask for comments from the interested parties. Only then will my superior and I decide what course of action to take."

"And you're the one who'll be doing the interviewing?"

"Presumably."

I had heard enough stories about a Kalliola much harder than the present soft demeanor indicated that I was curious to see what sort of tactics he'd adopt. If the CEO's secretary story held – and it was hard to see how it wouldn't – then Kalliola was in the worst jam of his civil-servant career, and he was well aware of it. Oksanen could hide behind Kalliola's broad back, and no doubt was doing so. After all, he'd acted with the blessing of a superior many links higher in the chain of command.

Kalliola's phone beeped, indicating an incoming text message. He fiddled with his smartphone and guffawed. "This is good. What do a Somali, a Russian, and a Finn do at the whorehouse? The Somali cleans, the Finn screws, and the Russian waits for his old lady to get off work."

When I didn't join in the revelry, Kalliola hurriedly shoved the phone back in his pocket. "Since we're playing with such high stakes here, I'd love to read what was written about me."

"Of course you'll be able to read the letter if this goes anywhere. But at first I need to find out what's been going on and who would be responsible for investigating, the National Bureau of Investigation or the prosecutor general."

Kalliola stopped breathing for a moment. "Come on, there's no way a ridiculous little thing like that can escalate to such levels. The media vultures will gorge themselves on it. All that would accomplish is damage to the organization as a whole, infinite damage." The furrows in Kalliola's forehead screamed disapproval.

"Like I said, first we'll look into it, and then we'll decide."

Kalliola smiled broadly, trying to chuckle. The laughter sounded more like the death rattle of a dying man. "I suppose you understand where this is going. The sense of proportion is all out of whack... and if I can be frank and split hairs, who's innocent enough to start throwing stones? Judge not lest ye be judged, says the big book. As I recall, your organization's magazine has more advertisements than stories, just like everyone else. There are more police magazines than our rally car has HP, and all of them are scrapping for advertising sales as fast as they can. That money is used for the good of police personnel, including clubs. What's the difference?"

It wasn't my job to defend the magazines or those who wrote them, which is why I said: "I'm not taking a stance on that, but if the magazines are violating the directives in the Police Act, then it's my understanding that it's the ministry's responsibility to intervene."

Now it was my phone's turn to ring. I silenced it, even though I saw the caller was Laurén's ex-wife.

Kalliola unconsciously slipped into the jargon he'd picked up at the ministry. "I can assure you that the matter has undergone thorough review, as the ministry has no desire to tarnish the unshakable trust the police force enjoys among the general public. We have, however, adopted a lenient policy, as it is our firm belief that all manner of leisure activity that meets legal and moral standards is of use in furthering the police force's capacity to carry out its demanding work. You must have a hobby, too, don't you? Golf, tennis, curling, sailing, opera, I love opera myself, models, diving —"

"I don't have any hobbies, at least nothing that would be subsidized through advertising sales in police magazines."

Kalliola momentarily lost his tongue. He raked his hand through his hair and looked off into the distance, as far as one could look inside a tent. Then he roused himself, the recipient of a fresh insight.

"One of our most active supporters is Lännen Osa. It's owned by Ruben Lasker. A very nice gentleman. Eats sausage just like everyone else without studying the ingredients too closely, and isn't a stickler when it comes to the Sabbath. He was very grateful when the department solved a break-in that had taken place at his warehouse. Got back a pretty significant haul. Maybe you ought to talk to him to form a more nuanced picture."

"Why?"

"Because he's one of you, a Jew."

"I know. So what?"

"Are you saying you believe his generous support of our club's activities makes him guilty of bribing a civil servant?"

"I don't know, and I don't care. If one of my subordinates accepts a bribe from him and someone reports it, I might care. A Jewish offender isn't going to get any sort of fellow Jew break from me."

"Just a moment…" Kalliola escaped into his cell phone again. He tapped at it for at least a minute before victoriously pressing the Send button.

"I was supposed to join the commissioner for a game of tennis at Taivallahti, but my back has been giving me trouble for a week. The wife gets to handle the business in bed while I just kick back and enjoy…" Kalliola's expression turned pained. "I went to this sports masseur I know yesterday, but the kinks still haven't worked themselves out… Highly recommended; it's the same guy who works on Mika Salo. Doesn't take new clients, but if I put in a good word…"

Kalliola scanned my face for any traces of empathy for his suffering. I satisfied myself with saying: "Sedentary work."

Kalliola's compass needle was spinning, searching for the right direction. In his experience, everyone had a string you could pull. He clearly didn't care for my attitude, but decided it was wiser not to show it. It wasn't worth angering me, at least not right now. Once this incident was safely behind him, he would have plenty of opportunity to pay me back, and with interest. I was setting myself up for future pain by irritating him.

"Oksanen and I have chatted about the department's attitude towards his rallying. He says everyone is supportive except you. He thinks you've decided to single him out because of it. Is that true?"

I nearly burst out laughing. Kalliola had turned our roles upside down; now he was the superior demanding explanations. I didn't answer, at which Kalliola scratched his earlobe.

"I was hoping there wasn't any sort of personal tinge involved."

"You can rest assured there isn't. Oksanen is into cars; another one of my subordinates is into Native American culture. It's all the same to me if they want to paint china, as long as it doesn't interfere with their work and doesn't lead to anything illegal."

A troop of heavily swathed Japanese women entered the tent and commandeered the bench. The salesperson stiffly hauled herself up out of her seat. Serving customers clearly was not a pleasure for her.

Kalliola crumpled up his paper cup and dropped it in the trash. "Your brother's a lawyer, isn't he?"

I conceded he was.

"And a competent one, too, they say… it's just I heard he was involved in an unfortunate incident where his business partner was shot. Am I remembering right?"

"More or less," I said, trying to figure out where Kalliola was going with this. His bringing up Eli was no accident.

"Things like that can eat at a man. How has he rebounded?"

"Well, as far as I understand."

Kalliola's forehead telegraphed that the kicker was coming. "A former colleague of mine is an inspector at the Security Police. He felt the case deserved closer examination. According to him, your brother's business partner was up to his ears in shady business affairs that bordered on treason."

"It's not too late," I said.

"You think you know someone, but you never do. People are a mystery, even to themselves."

I didn't understand what Kalliola meant, and he probably didn't either. He glanced at his watch. "Look at the time. This job is nothing but one meeting after another.

Fieldwork had its own pluses. I have to admit, sometimes I wish I were back on the streets… as a detective, shouldn't you be sitting at your desk instead of running around all the time?" Kalliola's tone wasn't inquisitive; it was critical.

"Things are more interesting out in the field."

"And evidently we'll meet again, once you've made some progress in your investigation."

Kalliola clearly hoped he would never set eyes on me again as long as he lived. He looked past me with a sour face, brusquely squeezed my hand, and left me to the company of the Japanese tourists.

I pulled up Seija Haapala's number and called her back the second I stepped out of the tent. I apologized for not having been able to answer.

"I promised to call if I heard anything. One of Reka's old friends from the Daybreak Academy called half an hour ago and asked if I knew how to get in touch with Reka. He's not answering his old number."

"Who was it who called?"

"Kai Halme, a bank manager from Turku… or I guess he lives in Helsinki these days. I have his number."

I wrote the number down.

"Did he say anything else, like why he was trying to reach Laurén?"

"Only that Reka had tried to call him a while back but that he hadn't been able to take the call at the moment and then the whole thing had slipped his mind. When he remembered, the number said it was out of service."

"Have you met this Halme before?"

"It's been almost fifteen years, probably. He was at business school then. He came to the housewarming party at our first place… or I guess I ran into him at some event since then, but that was years ago."

"Was he a member of the Sacred Vault, too?"

"I'm pretty sure. I remember them talking about it when they were drunk."

"And you didn't remember last time we talked?"

"You can't remember everything," Seija snapped.

I thanked her for the information. "And Laurén hasn't called you?"

My surprise question didn't catch Haapala off guard. She laughed softly. "If he had, I would have told you."

"What about your daughter?"

"Now that I don't know."

12

Stenman had finally managed to get hold of Laurén's daughter and set up a meeting at police HQ. She called that afternoon to let me know the girl was in the lobby. I asked Stenman to bring her to the conference room.

The daughter took after Laurén in looks, after her mother in style. She was seventeen, but looked older. Her outfit consisted of a hippie-style skirt, light-green knee-length coat in a military cut, and well-worn brown leather boots. A hand-knitted rainbow scarf was wrapped around her neck.

As she flung her coat down on the chair next to her, I sensed a reticence about meeting with me.

"I'm sure your mother told you why we need information on your father," I began.

"No. Or at least I didn't get what she was trying to tell me. I guess he's lost it somehow, but I don't get why that means I have to come in and be interrogated."

Stenman corrected her: "This isn't an interrogation, this is a chat."

"It sure seems like an interrogation."

"We're looking for him because we want to make sure he isn't planning on doing anything to himself or anyone else. You don't want your dad ending up in trouble, do you?"

The girl pulled off her scarf, which was wrapped around her throat at least three times. "You guys don't have anything to be afraid of. He would never hurt anyone, at least not anyone else. It's against his principles. He's the biggest softie I know."

"Softie dads usually stay in touch with their only daughters," Stenman noted.

"Yeah, he calls and texts me sometimes."

"When was the last time?"

"Yesterday." The girl reached into her woven shoulder bag, pulled out her cell phone, and studied it for a moment. "'Good night, sweetheart. Sweet dreams. Love, Dad.' Hope that helps." As she read the message, a tenderness bordering on tears colored the girl's voice.

"What number did the message come from?"

I glanced at the number. It was the same one Laurén had called me from earlier. "Does he have any other phone numbers?"

"He's had this one for at least six months."

"Can you tell us where your father might be?"

"If he's not at home then I don't know where he is."

"At the apartment in Töölö, you mean?"

"Yeah. Dad has lived there for a year or so. He inherited the place from some old aunt."

"Your father hasn't been there for several days now. Do you know if he has an RV?"

"If he does, he never showed it to me. He always talked about getting one, said we'd go off and drive around Finland together."

"Where do you live yourself?" Stenman asked.

"I have a place with a couple of friends —"

"You're pretty young to be on your own."

"It's better than being at home."

"You and your mom don't get along?"

"Show me someone who does."

"You're still in high school. Where do you get rent money?"

"Dad. He also inherited a bunch of money and stocks. He sold them right away. Said he's not cut out to be a stock-market speculator." Mandi smiled for the first time. She probably didn't even notice. "Mom pretends to be so artistic and bohemian, but she's really not. Dad is. If he has money, he'll give it to anyone who bothers to ask. Dad's old friends take advantage of his generosity."

This gave me a good way in: "Do you think he might be staying with one of his old friends?"

"The only one I know is Ola Sotamaa. And him only because he's famous, at least sort of, and he's been to our place a few times. He has his own radio show."

"He said the last time he saw your dad was six months ago."

"Could be. Dad has been pretty mysterious and spending lots of time alone… But Ola has been to our place since then… because of Mom."

"Are they dating?" Stenman asked.

"No. Maybe Ola wants to, but Mom doesn't."

"Did your father ever tell you about the Brotherhood of the Sacred Vault he belonged to in boarding school?"

"Yeah. Mom laughed at that stuff. I thought it was exciting. I liked hearing about Dad when he was young, even though it was a hundred years ago... not quite, I guess."

"What did he tell you?"

"That they wanted to make the world a better place by ridding the Church of hypocrisy and stuff like that. When he was young, Dad wanted to be a pastor, but he changed his mind at Daybreak. Dad said it opened his eyes to all of the evil that's done in the name of good."

"Did he say what he meant?" Stenman asked.

"He hated the fact that religious people were greedy, stingy, and self-absorbed, even though the Bible taught modesty and generosity. He said that the Church is full of Pharisees that follow the letter of the law but not its spirit."

"Did your dad ever see his Sacred Vault friends? Or did he mention them by name?"

"No. Or once. They were interviewing some bishop on TV and Dad turned it off, because he didn't want to hear anything that two-faced shit had to say. I asked him what he meant. Dad said the bishop had been in the Sacred Vault with him but had broken all his promises once he rose to a position of power in the Church."

"Do you remember the bishop's name?"

"No. It was a couple of years ago."

"Would you recognize him if we looked at pictures of bishops together?" Stenman opened the laptop she had with her. A moment later she found what she was looking for and set the computer down in front of Mandi.

It only took twenty seconds for Mandi to spot the right man. "That's the guy. I remember him from the ears and bald head and glasses."

I glanced at the picture. Mandi had identified one of the younger bishops, who appeared relatively often on TV. He was generally considered liberal.

"You guys need anything else?" Mandi asked, and stood up.

I stood up, too. "Your dad has called me several times. I've noticed how important you are to him. I hope you'll help us find him and get in touch right away if you hear anything so things will go well for him."

Mandi's early-adult walls came crashing down. She held back the tears as she spoke: "Don't let Dad do anything he'll go to prison for... he's been through so much already. You guys have to help him..."

I promised to do my best. Stenman escorted her to the lobby.

My phone had been on silent during my meeting with Mandi; I'd missed three incoming calls. Now it rang again. I heard a decisive female voice: "This is Ritva Somero. I asked for Detective Oksanen and the switchboard put me through to you. I'm calling from the Daybreak Academy. Detective Oksanen was asking about former employees a couple of days ago. Did I reach the right person?"

"Yes. Oksanen is on sick leave. I'm his superior."

"I'm calling because I think I unintentionally provided him with some incorrect information. I told him we have never had anyone named Leo Anteroinen on the payroll. As it turns out Anteroinen did work here, but his name was recorded as Kalevi Leo Anteroinen, not Leo Kalevi Anteroinen. We knew him here as Kalevi, or Kale. That's why the Leo didn't ring any bells, although of course it should have. After speaking with Detective Oksanen, I did some double-checking and discovered my mistake. Apparently he's the individual Detective Oksanen was referring to."

"So Leo Anteroinen was a former employee of the Academy?"

"He worked here from the spring of 1976 to the summer of 1980. I didn't start here until 1979. I was just filling in initially, which is why I never got to know him very well."

"What was his position at Daybreak?"

"He was a custodian or maintenance man; as far as I'm concerned, it's the same thing."

That settled the matter. It was the right Anteroinen. We had our first connection. The Daybreak Academy. It linked Laurén to Anteroinen.

"Is there anything else you can tell me about him?"

"Very little. I discussed the matter with Headmaster Hätönen, and he was exceedingly interested as to why the police were asking about Daybreak's former employees. He's sensitive about our reputation and, I suppose, leery of the academy getting mixed up in negative publicity."

"We're investigating matters relating to his death."

I heard a gasp. "I didn't know Kalevi had died. Was there a crime involved?"

"That's what we're investigating," I lied. I was eager to get down to the matter at hand.

"What do you mean by 'anything else'? I didn't know him well, barely at all."

"What was he like? Where did he come from, and why did he leave? Anything you can tell us is valuable."

"As I recall, he was from the west coast, maybe southern Ostrobothnia. He lived in the staff quarters, was a bachelor. Rather quiet and antisocial. I might be mistaken, because he and I didn't have much to do with each other. He made sure the drives were plowed, the roads were sanded, the radiators stayed warm, and so on. I usually saw him in the canteen at lunch, and occasionally at academy events."

"Do you remember if there was anyone on the staff who was on good terms with Anteroinen?"

"There might have been, but I wouldn't know. Maybe one of the younger teachers or youth counselors. They were a pretty carefree bunch; they all lived in the same building."

"Daybreak has a religious mission."

"Yes, but we employed all sorts of people. Not all of them were religious, and I don't suppose these days you could legally require them to be. Headmaster Kivalo was a pastor by training and probably genuinely religious, but he was – if I can be frank – a rather lax, timid man and didn't intervene in the affairs of the staff. He lived with his family in a separate building, and probably wasn't aware of what went on in the staff quarters."

"What went on there?"

"Young people are the same everywhere. They partied the way they do everywhere else."

"In the student dorms as well?"

"Yes. Many of the boys were already in high school, after all. Got their hands on alcohol somehow, even though they were underage... maybe from the staff."

Something about Ms. Somero's voice prompted me to probe further. "Was Anteroinen the one who bought it for them?"

"I don't like to form opinions on the basis of gossip, but that was the rumor."

"Is that the reason he had to leave the academy?"

"Among others."

"I want to know every detail. I don't want to filter anything out." My voice was so stern it instantly did the trick.

"There was some sort of scandal... as a result, the father of one of the students demanded that Anteroinen be fired or he would bring in the police. Of course, that spooked Headmaster Kivalo, as timid as he was, because the father was an influential figure, owned his own construction company and was a major donor to Daybreak. But the rumor was that Anteroinen was a scapegoat."

"What do you mean by scandal?"

"Oh dear, oh dear. These are such unpleasant matters... I'll be retiring soon and I don't want any trouble..."

"Like Headmaster Kivalo?" It was a nasty jab, but it worked.

"One of the students, the son of this construction company owner, claimed that Anteroinen had touched him inappropriately in the gymnasium showers."

"Was he the only one?"

"The only one who complained… but if you have such tendencies, you're not likely to stop at one."

"What was the boy's name?"

"Providing names is a little delicate for us, and we're not sure —"

"I want the boy's name, and also the full list of students Detective Oksanen requested."

After a brief silence, I heard an uneasy voice again. "The principal doesn't feel that this is information the police automatically have a right to, or at least that we'd need to know first what sort of investigation is involved."

"What could there be to hide in student rosters?"

"Nothing, perhaps, but Headmaster Hätönen feels we can't just hand them over regardless. It would be best if you would contact him directly."

"Let's do it that way, then. I also want a list of academy staff from the period in question."

"Some are already deceased."

"In any event. And I'm sure you can give me Headmaster Kivalo's information right off the bat."

"I'm afraid it won't do you much good. He's one of the deceased."

"When did he die?"

"About three years ago now."

"How did it happen?"

"What? The death?"

"Exactly."

"Some sort of accident, as far as I know… in Spain. By the time he had left us he was a widower. He moved to the Costa del Sol."

"What sort of accident? A car accident?"

"It might have been. I don't know the details. As I recall, I heard about it from Headmaster Hätönen… he just said accident. I think it was mentioned during one of our morning devotionals."

"Does the Sacred Vault mean anything to you?"

"Detective Oksanen asked about that, too. I told him I'd heard rumors about it, but nothing solid. It was said that the boys from one of the high-school classes had founded a secret society that met in the dorms at night."

"Do you know any of the members by name?"

"At least the boy you mentioned."

"Laurén?"

"Yes."

"Evidently you remember him clearly?"

"That's because… this is another one of those things you should speak to the headmaster about."

"I'm not asking these questions for my amusement, or out of curiosity. We're conducting an investigation of a serious crime and trying to prevent the commission of future crimes. If something ends up happening, you will bear partial responsibility."

I was exaggerating a little, I had to admit, but I was starting to get fed up with Ms. Somero's beating around the bush.

When she answered, her voice sounded almost teary. "I'd like to help, but the headmaster said in no uncertain terms I was to —"

"I'm going to ask the headmaster the same questions, and I won't say a peep about you."

"Do I have your word? I don't want to get in trouble during my final months here. I'm retiring in early June and…" I could almost see her struggling with herself.

"You can rest assured I won't mention you."

"Reijo was a very nice boy, but extremely sensitive and unstable and had a lot of problems with his parents… his father. He was a gifted and musical boy, played in the academy orchestra. Everyone liked him. That's why it was so sad for all of us."

"What?"

"His suicide attempt. He tried to hang himself, but the other boys got him down in time. He was gone from Daybreak for a month, then his father brought him back. The father seemed like a hard man, the black-and-white type. He knew Headmaster Kivalo well. I almost felt sorry for the boy…"

13

RITUAL

Session of the Service's Guardians of Highest Wisdom

LOCATION: *Temple of the Vault, boys' dorm fourth floor*
PRESENT: *Great Guardian of Souls (highest-ranking member)*
                Guardian of the Great Seal (scribe)
                Adorner of the Sacred Vault (convener)

Three magi have been made highest officers of the Vault through the sacred seals that are collectively known as the Gospel of the Three Angels. God is an ever-present principle in the three worlds. According to the strictures of the Vault, anyone who betrays his brothers will be utterly banished from our fraternity for a period of thirty years, which symbolizes the thirty pieces of silver for which Judas betrayed his Lord.

We kneel on the floor of the temple in the shape of an intertwined triangle, forming a golden pyramid of wisdom, love, and service. We wear white garb reminiscent of the ceremonial robes of the high priest of ancient Israel, covering the heart, the breast, and the upper abdomen. Each of us holds in our hands a coded message that each of us has decoded and which must be identical in order for the Holy Ceremony to take place. Thirty-three hours after the decision is made, evil will be brought before the eternal high judge to suffer its horrific fate.

Each of us has sworn a sacred vow that we will not give up before evil has been avenged and excised from this world. We are angels of vengeance, servants of truth, who carry out the will of the Lord.

We have sealed this Holy Vow with our own blood.

The description of the ritual was written on a page cut out from a diary. At the bottom was a date written in ballpoint pen: March 26, 1979.

I had received mail from Laurén again. He clearly wanted to crack open the door to his world, but only a little at a time. The most troubling thing was that even though the passage was old, it contained a violent threat. It felt odd to think that high-school boys would have seriously considered killing someone. The more likely scenario was that it was a thrilling game, like spiritism at confirmation camp.

The envelope had contained that sole diary page, nothing more. No signature, and no hint as to the message's purpose or significance.

I remembered Laurén had used the title Adorner of the Sacred Vault in reference to himself. So he was the convener responsible for practical arrangements. Of the three leaders of the Vault, he probably held the lowest rank. Above him were the Guardian of the Great Seal and above all was the Great Guardian of Souls. If the Sacred Vault was hierarchical, did Laurén do anything without the permission of the Great Guardian of Souls? Might the Great Guardian be the accomplice? Somehow it felt as if Laurén, as unhinged as he was, could not have been solely responsible for three unsolved murders. He was by no means stupid, but getting away with one murder in Finland was hard enough, let alone three.

On the other hand, it was hard to imagine that two other leaders of the Sacred Vault were, now, at the age of forty, so far gone that they'd still be playing at a secret society. Cowboys and Indians and cops and robbers were generally left behind by early adolescence.

Well, maybe not for everyone. Simolin still played Indians. At gatherings attended by others with similar interests, he wore a fringed buckskin suit, beaded moccasins, and a feathered headdress, and used an Indian name he refused to reveal to his colleagues, despite numerous inquiries.

Sometimes serendipity toys with you in a way verging on the miraculous. There was a knock at the door. I waited for whoever it was to enter without being asked. When there was no sign of my visitor, I said: "Come in."

I saw Simolin's apologetic face peering in. "I just dropped by and —"

"I thought you were supposed to be in Canada?"

"Change of plans. My trip got cut short by a week… I hear you have an unusual case on your hands… Arja told me. I can give you a hand if —"

"You still have vacation time left."

"I can postpone it till winter. That actually works better."

"Then there couldn't be a better time. Arja and I have been tackling this alone."

Simolin was one of those meek of the earth you missed most when they weren't around. When they were present, they worked efficiently and without making a big spectacle of themselves.

"Then I'll go ahead and start right away."

I gave Simolin a brief account of everything I knew. I finished by showing him the diary page I had just received. He was brimming with enthusiasm. I boosted his motivation by saying: "Based on what Laurén has told us, we can assume there's more revenge to come. In the letter he talks about five evils, but there have only been three bodies, at least that we're aware of, assuming Headmaster Kivalo is part of the count. We need to figure out who might be next on the list. We'll never hear the end of it if someone else is killed and it turns out we've been suspecting Laurén but weren't able to prevent another murder."

"No doubt. Why don't I have a word with Silén's wife? I'll try to find some connection to the other cases. There has to be something. Why else would Laurén be interested in him? On top of everything else, Silén is a corporate lawyer."

I approved his suggestion with a nod.

"Arja told me that Jari is on sick leave."

"His back is acting up."

Simolin was a naif, and it never occurred to him that anything else might be involved. He accepted my reply and dropped the matter then and there.

"Laurén's ex-wife suspected that he might have access to an RV. Can you also look into whether you can find anything on that?"

Simolin made himself a note. Now it read *RV* in his notebook, too.

"You could also try and find Laurén's friends from boarding school. They must know something about the Sacred Vault and its members. There's only one original employee left at Daybreak, and she's about to retire. It won't hurt to have you call her again and hurry her to send the student rosters. You can also ask her about employees who have retired or left the academy."

Simolin conscientiously wrote down my suggestions like the maître d' at a fine-dining establishment making a note of a customer's wishes. When he realized that was all, he exited, barely able to contain his eagerness.

I ordered myself a pepperoni pizza from the nearest pizzeria. I got halfway through it before my lunch was interrupted by a phone call. I immediately recognized the voice.

"Did you get my letter?"

"I did, thanks. I just don't understand what it is you're trying to say —"

"I want to initiate you into the mysteries of the Sacred Vault. No other outsiders know anything about them."

"I appreciate the gesture, but why me exactly?"

"I thought I already told you. You've been chosen, just as we have. You're the Flame of God that will burn evil to ashes."

"I'm not a flame, I'm a cop."

When Laurén didn't respond, I was afraid I'd made a mistake. Maybe it would be better to play along instead of being a smart aleck. You could never tell with crazy people, or should I say the psychologically infirm.

"Everything has a purpose, even the little things. You might not understand it yet, but you're part of a grand plan. I'm part of it too, along with the other… brothers of the Vault."

I tried my luck: "How many were there of you again…?"

"I'm only speaking on my own behalf."

"Have you committed any other murders, aside from Anteroinen, Sandberg, and Kivalo?"

Kivalo was a long shot, but Laurén didn't flinch. "They weren't murders; they were justice. They died for their misdeeds; they sentenced themselves to death."

"What evil did Kivalo commit?"

"Every one of them sinned and earned death —"

"We've gathered all the information we can get our hands on, but to me these killings are still murders. Wouldn't it be easier if you told us the reason now? Why do you think they're justice?"

"Everything will unfold in a prescribed order, and now is not the time. You'll come to learn that, too. We are treading the same path, me ahead, you behind."

"No matter what the reason is, in Finland if you kill another human being you'll be called to account. Have you considered that?"

Now Laurén sounded almost surprised. "Apparently you've accepted the simplest interpretation for what has happened. The fact that I know about the incidents doesn't mean that I killed them."

"I'm pretty sure anybody would have arrived at the same conclusion. In any case, you believe Anteroinen, Sandberg, and Kivalo are guilty of something, as a result of which they deserve death. Isn't that true?"

Laurén's voice was as shrill as a hacksaw running across a chain. "They got off easy. I said now is not the time to discuss it."

"What about Silén, what evil did Henry Silén do to you?"

"Who?"

"Attorney at law Henry Silén."

"What makes you think I've done anything to him?"

"He's been missing for two months, since about the time you asked your college buddy Sotamaa about him."

"Oh, him," Laurén said insouciantly. "That was something else. Once you find out what kind of man he is, you won't be surprised he disappeared, but I'm pretty sure he did it voluntarily."

"So what kind of man is he, and what has he done?"

"As an officer of the law you should know. I've heard that there are quite a few people wondering where their money went, but I didn't call you to discuss such worldly trivialities."

"I see. What did you call to discuss, then? Shall we talk about your girlfriend Roosa Nevala? Maybe in this context it's inaccurate to use the word 'sense,' but I'll use it anyway. What sense did it make to steal her body?"

"She suggested it herself. She wanted to die, and it was the only way she could participate. She said it would open everyone's eyes and get them to understand how serious we are. She also wanted me to burn her body."

"Sometimes you speak in the singular, other times in the plural. So there's more than one of you?"

Laurén didn't take the bait.

"Your daughter Mandi came by today to see us. We had a long chat. She's worried about you and asked us to make sure you don't come to harm. She said she wouldn't be able to stand it if you ended up in prison."

After a moment's silence, Laurén said: "Mandi is a wonderful girl. Luckily her mother hasn't been able to completely poison her against me. The only reason I called this time is to propose an exchange. I'll tell you more about Anteroinen if you acquire a certain address for me."

I nearly retorted that I wasn't an address service or a phone book, but I managed to restrain myself. Instead, I played my latest card. "I already know everything I need to know about Anteroinen. He was a pedophile who molested boys at Daybreak."

There was a long silence at the other end of the line. "Anteroinen was a little rat who did what the big rats told him to."

I came back to Laurén's request: "Depends on whose address it is you want and why."

"The name is Vesa Särkijärvi. I need his address in Finland. He lives in Brussels and used to be my teacher. I'd like to write him."

"I can't promise, but I can try. Tell me a little more about the Sacred Vault. So you were the convener."

Laurén improved his title: "The Adorner of the Sacred Vault."

"Who was the Great Guardian of Souls?"

"I'll tell you about the Vault in general terms, but I can't give you any names other than my own. I took a blood oath."

"Why not? You guys were practically children then, and now you're adults. The oath doesn't mean anything anymore."

"Just the opposite. It means everything. It's as valid today as it was thirty years ago. There's one critical thing you still haven't grasped: for us, the Brotherhood of the Sacred Vault still exists."

14

When it comes down to it, "bank manager" is a pretty hazy concept, especially for the generation that was introduced to the profession through the Happy Families card deck. I had to admit I wasn't sure if loans were granted by a bank manager these days or a computer algorithm that assessed the applicant's debt load.

I suppose Halme was, to be precise, head of the bank's corporate banking division, which made it easy to reach him.

He didn't sound surprised that I'd contacted him. We agreed to meet at his workplace. People of his status generally wanted to meet elsewhere.

The conference room looked like exactly that: a long table, a dozen or so chairs, a flip chart, and a laptop through which one could relay the latest growth projections in tidied-up Excel format onto a flat-screen TV. In honor of our visit – Simolin and myself were in attendance – there were coffees, sweet rolls, and mineral water.

"Help yourselves," Halme said, indicating the basket of sweet rolls as he poured us coffee from the thermos.

Halme was a big man with rugged features and dark hair that was starting to gray. I couldn't help thinking that he was the sort of boss who would have a penchant for affairs with luscious secretaries while his adoring wife waited at home. He was shirt-model handsome in the same way as Huovinen. I noticed the insignia for the Finnish Club, Finland's answer to British gentlemen's clubs, on the lapel of his navy-blue blazer. That fit the picture, too.

"You're not the first police officers to pay us a visit," he said, with a glance at a row of pennants on the windowsill. The insignia of both the Finnish Security Intelligence Service and the lion-head pennant of the Helsinki Police Association stood there. The pennants were generally given as a token of appreciation for generous and generously lubricated hosting.

"You said you wanted to ask about my old schoolmate, Reka Laurén. Did you hear about me from his wife? I guess it doesn't matter. At first I thought this was about drugs – Reka used to mess around with them – but then I punched your name into a search engine and it turns out that you work in homicide… I have to say, I'm curious."

"We're looking for him, so any and all information is useful."

"Likewise. I'm looking for him, too; I suppose his wife – or ex-wife – told you."

"Why?"

"Why does anyone look for an old friend… I got divorced, moved here from Turku a while back, and thought it would be nice to see him. I tried to call his old number but couldn't get through. That's as far as my search got, not that I've tried very hard since then. So I don't think I'll be much help."

"When was the last time you saw him?" Simolin asked.

"Maybe about a year ago. We met while I was here in Helsinki on business. It was good seeing him. I guess he was in a good place at the time; I know there have been bad ones, too. I suppose you might already be aware of the problems…"

Halme's inquisitive glance lobbed the ball into our court. I didn't return it.

"Go on."

"About the problems?"

"Sure."

"It would help if I knew what you were looking for… what is Reka suspected of?"

"We'd like to speak with him personally about some things. But you guys used to talk on the phone now and again?"

"A few times after we met… that's why I'm a little worried…"

We didn't need to ask; Halme knew we were expecting him to continue.

"Maybe it will help you understand if I shared a little about our history. We attended the Daybreak Academy together in high school. It's a Christian prep school with roots in the States. Our parents were religious, like those of most of the other students. That was the main reason families wanted to send their kids there… am I going back too far?"

I encouraged him to continue.

"Reka's parents, or at least his dad, were even stricter than mine. He didn't get any support from his family when he ran into problems. Just the opposite; it drove them further apart. Reka and I were in the same class and got along well. Both of us were musical. I played violin and he played piano and guitar. We performed at school parties together a few times —"

The phone on the desk rang and Halme answered. "Tell them to wait... or tell Pekka to go ahead and start things up and go first. I'm going to be here a while yet... staff training, nothing more critical than that... So Reka and I got along pretty well. The problems began during our second year. At that point, someone I've actively been trying to forget joined the staff as a youth counselor. Remembering him is repellent —"

"What's his name?" Simolin asked.

"Vesa Särkijärvi. He'd been trained at the original Daybreak in the States; I guess that's why he had much higher status at the academy than his position warranted. On top of that, he knew how to manipulate people, pinpoint their weaknesses, pull their strings. He'd also earned a degree in music pedagogy in the States. That meant we spent a lot of time with him."

I remembered Laurén having asked for this Särkijärvi's address.

Halme shot us another glance and said: "I'll try to get to the point. It wasn't long before we started hearing all sorts of things about Särkijärvi. The older boys joked that you didn't want to end up practicing with Särkijärvi after school."

I saw Simolin's forehead furrow in concentration.

"Pretty soon we discovered all the stories were true. Särkijärvi's interest in little boys turned out to be not so healthy."

"So you're saying he was a pedophile?" Simolin asked.

"That's putting it mildly. When I've thought back on his behavior, I've realized he knew all the tricks of the trade. He was a good buddy, took you under his wing, bought you candy, ice cream, helped you with your homework, talked to you, listened to your worries. That was the feeling-out phase, when he would decide whether the kid was susceptible. If you could be coaxed with treats so much the better, but if not, his MO changed. He'd come up with made-up accusations, say, threaten to tell your parents you'd been drinking, masturbating, shoplifting from the canteen, or anything else that was anathema to a religious family and would bring shame down on the boy himself. At some point Särkijärvi set his sights on Reka. He asked Reka to stay late to practice this one piece of music that wasn't going very well. The academy was in a different building than the dorms, so it was generally empty at night, especially on weekends, when a lot of the kids went home. Think about it. Alone in an empty building with a pedophile. I have to say, it sends shivers up my spine to this day when I think about him."

Thinking about it sent shivers up my spine, too.

"Was he the only pedophile at Daybreak?"

Halme shook his head. "That's what made it so much worse. The custodian was this creepy guy named Anteroinen. He closed the doors, turned off the lights, made sure the heating system was working. Daybreak had a boiler room that burned both wood and oil. It was in the basement. At first I heard the older boys talking about a boiler-room gig. I didn't know what it meant, but it became clear in time. When Särkijärvi felt he'd gotten far along enough with a boy, sunk his claws into him, he'd take him down to the boiler room under some pretense. Anteroinen would unlock the door and act as lookout. For his troubles, he got to peek in through the crack in the door and watch. Evidently he got a bigger kick out of that than doing anything himself. The guy had this rat-like quality to him, even though he was big and strong as a gorilla."

I remembered what Laurén had said about a little rat.

"What did Headmaster Kivalo do? Did he know what was going on?"

"Definitely. A few boys wrote him an anonymous letter. But he didn't do anything. He was a mouse of a man, was afraid a scandal would bring down Daybreak, and him with it. He knew a similar incident had come out at the US church in the past. That had been swept under the rug, too, so there wouldn't have been any help coming from America, just the opposite. That meant Reka and a few of the other boys had to pay the price for Särkijärvi's shenanigans. Reka wasn't able to talk about it with anyone, not even me, and in the end he tried to kill himself. That failed, too. He was sent home on sick leave for a couple of months, but he came back. So I'm not too surprised that he developed psychological problems later." Halme looked at his watch, but I pretended not to take the hint.

"The students had a fraternity called the Sacred Vault. Did you belong to it?"

Halme chuckled. "Yes. Where did you hear about that? It's still a big secret. Anyone who talked about it was supposed to have his tongue cut out and be banished for thirty years."

"What was its aim? Every organization has a mission."

"Yeah, we did, too, and it wasn't exactly modest. Our goal was to go into different fields and gradually take over the Finnish Lutheran Church and rebuild it from the ground up. I planned on studying theology myself. Let me tell you, the world lost a real preacher in me. We were walking in the footsteps of Martin Luther and as serious as only kids that age can be. The Vault had been founded before we arrived at Daybreak, but the mission hadn't changed. On the side, we planned Särkijärvi's murder and getting rid of his body in the furnace. We didn't do that either, unfortunately."

"Who planned it?"

"At least me, Reka, Jukka Majavuori, Moisio, and Jokela. It was Jokela's idea. He promised to throw Särkijärvi into the furnace himself if need be. It never went beyond talk."

"What were Jokela's and Moisio's first names?"

"Tuomo – we called him Tonto – and Heikki."

"Weren't all three of them equally guilty, Särkijärvi, Anteroinen, and Kivalo?"

"Not just three. We were all guilty, I mean all of us who knew but didn't have the courage to do anything about it. It took me a long time before I could look myself in the face. We were as guilty as villagers living near a concentration camp who smelled the reek of burning bodies but convinced themselves that the smoke was nothing more than burning garbage."

"Someone had the courage to kill Anteroinen, though."

"I read about that in the paper. The case was never solved, right? It's not nice to say, but it served the creep right... That's not why you're looking for Reka, is it? A guy like that is going to have plenty of enemies, so that's pretty far-fetched. I heard Anteroinen was hanging out with unsavory elements."

I continued without commenting. "Someone also killed Headmaster Kivalo."

"That was a robbery in Spain. You can rest assured the Sacred Vault didn't have anything to do with those murders. We were kids looking for meaning for their lives, a little mysticism and excitement. We weren't any worse than Boy Scouts. We didn't murder anyone then, and even less now."

"But you planned it."

"At that age, you come up with all sorts of things. None of us were serious. It was make-believe. Moisio came up with the idea of luring Särkijärvi into the boiler room and shoving him into the furnace. It could take three-foot logs. Evil would have gotten its reward."

"Pretty brutal plans."

Halme didn't seem to hear. He was still lost in his memories. "I can still remember the smell of that boiler room: smoke, drying wood, oil, grime. The boiler made this clicking sound, the gauges clinked, and the air was thrumming. Smelling that smell still makes me want to puke."

"What is Särkijärvi doing now?"

"When the whispers and rumors started spreading, he was awarded a scholarship and sent back to the States to continue his studies. Church policy; they wanted to cover up any tracks. At some point, Särkijärvi came back to Finland and got a doctorate in theology. Last I heard, he was in Brussels on some special EU assignment. He probably still is. No one has murdered him. The statute of limitations on his crimes passed years ago... it would still make for a good news story if —"

"If what?"

"There's a recording that proves what Särkijärvi was up to... Moisio hid a tape recorder in the boiler room and set it up so Reka would turn it on the next time Särkijärvi brought him down there. It worked, but Moisio held on to the tape."

"Why?"

"Maybe he started being afraid they'd figure out whose tape recorder and idea it had been. I was there when he listened to the tape. It turned out surprisingly well. Every word is crystal clear. It was damned creepy. Well, Moisio is long gone, and I'm guessing the tape is, too."

"Laurén belonged to the Sacred Vault, too, didn't he?" Simolin asked.

"Of course. There were about twenty members. New members joined and the old ones moved on once they graduated."

"I'd like all of their names," I said.

"It's been almost thirty years. I can't remember all of them."

"As many as you can remember."

"I've got to get to this staff training, so I suggest I take my time thinking at home tonight, make a couple of phone calls, and get the names to you tomorrow. I have a class photo somewhere, too. It might help me remember. Does that work?"

I said it did. Halme was already standing up when I asked one final question: "Who were the Great Guardian of Souls, the Guardian of the Great Seal, and the Adorner of the Sacred Vault?"

"Tonto, I mean Jokela, Jukka Majavuori, and Reka, in that order."

"Where can I find Jokela and Majavuori?"

Halme pointed upwards. It took a moment for the gesture to register.

"Majavuori's dead. Shot himself. Was a successful surgeon. You can pin that one on Särkijärvi, too. Majavuori was one of his victims who could never completely free himself from his past. He wasn't the only one. Two other former Vaulters killed themselves, too, a couple have become junkies, a few are drunks. Some have psychological problems. Others are successful and at the pinnacle of society, judges, lawyers, politicians, doctors, scientists, captains of industry. They're not interested in rebuilding the Finnish Lutheran Church, though."

"I'm guessing you aren't either," I said.

"No, I have to say I'm not. I'd rather rebuild the business world, if that. It's even more stuck in its ways than the Church."

"Not even Johan Kaltio, who was named bishop a year ago? He also belonged to the Vault, didn't he?"

"Oh, yeah, that's right. Reka expected a lot from him and was badly disappointed. His brand of rebuilding was supporting the sort of change favored by progressives." Halme gave the word *progressives* another meaning by putting it in air quotes.

"So Reka feels God shouldn't adapt to meet man's preferences, but that man should adapt to those eternal forms God has laid out for him."

Halme gave me a quizzical look. "Would Judaism have survived if the old religious and cultural traditions were always done away with just because the new generation wasn't feeling them? Move the Sabbath to Tuesday and shorten it to two hours, toss out kosher guidelines because they get in the way of living a normal life and offend pork eaters? And Pesach would of course be turned into a celebration for all religions of the world."

"I think I'll leave that unanswered, but I know what you mean."

"Anyway, Reka tore into Kaltio right after his acceptance speech and broke off all contact with him."

Simolin came back to the original question. "What about Jokela?"

"He went off to Germany to study and came back a couple of years ago... pretty strange coincidence, but I heard just a week ago that he's lying in a coma in

Tampere. Overdose… there's nothing funny going on there. The way he was going, it's a miracle it didn't happen earlier."

"What did Laurén mean when he told me that the Brotherhood of the Vault still exists?"

"I have no idea. Maybe that a lot of them have held on to their ideals from that time. The Vault shriveled up and died back in the '80s."

"Do you stay in touch with its former members?" Simolin asked.

"Not really. I might run into one of them somewhere and have a couple of beers, remember old times. When Daybreak celebrated its ninetieth anniversary, I attended. There were a few members of the Vault there. I guess the next time we'll see each other is when Daybreak celebrates another decade; it's turning 100 at the end of April."

The question had been lingering in the air, so I finally asked it. "How did you fare with Särkijärvi?"

"Better than most. My dad was a cop, and I threatened to tell him when Särkijärvi tried to fondle me. That did the trick. He left me alone. It still bothers me that I didn't have the courage to come forward about Särkijärvi and the other boys… But now I have to get going. We'll have to get back to this later."

We rose at the same time as Halme. "Get us those names."

"I'm still not sure what it is you want with Reka."

"I'm not surprised, because I'm not sure myself."

15

I'd only recently started to understand the meaning of family in our lives. My brother Eli had been selling me on it for twenty years, but who listens to their older brother? At least not to an older brother whose marriage, despite a handsome facade that included a luxurious home in Helsinki's poshest district, Eira, was a mass of complications. Eli had cheated on his wife Silja with his co-worker Max's wife Ruth on the leather sofa of his office, and Silja had cheated to get back at him. The kids had survived, however; both of them were at the university. The old married couple had also accepted that their coexistence wasn't perfect but better than the alternative.

I didn't ask for much from life. A one-bedroom apartment, comfortable furniture, a good stereo, a few modern works painted by my artist cousin, and a four-figure sum in my bank account were enough for me. I had little in the way of material possessions, but no debt either. I enjoyed living in Punavuori, where I'd spent my entire life. My dad had been born there, too. Every old building, park, hill, and slab of shoreline granite brought back memories, if I chose to remember. My dad had owned a dilapidated fishing boat that smelled of mold and petrol and was kept down at the Kaivopuisto marina. In the spring, Dad would fix it up alongside the other men, moor it between the dock posts, and there it would stay right up until the autumn storms came and it was time to haul it out for winter. The boat had a butane stove we would cook on from time to time; Dad would even fry up any fish Eli and I managed to catch.

All I asked for was a good woman, and with that I was asking for everything. It had been two years since my previous dalliance, which with some goodwill one could have characterized as dating. Now and then I paid a visit to a nice Russian woman who lived a couple of blocks away and sponsored her teenage children's education. That relationship cost me €150 a pop. It was a steal.

After one such visit, I had literally taken a good look at myself in the mirror. Was I so stuck in my pitiful bachelor ways that I couldn't stand another person with their own ways at my side? I wanted to challenge my doubts. Someone else's toothbrush in the bathroom or a roll of toilet paper hanging the wrong way didn't bother me. What made me anxious was the thought that once we started living together, all of my comings and goings would be somehow subject to that other person's will. If I wanted to go out for a beer after work, I would have to take into consideration that someone was expecting me at home, maybe even that that someone had cooked a dinner for me that would get cold if I didn't show up on time.

Despite such restless ruminations, I was even more anxious about being alone. In my desperation, I had started attending community events in the hopes that a few lusty widows or divorcees would have somehow found their way there. And I had met one two weeks ago, but after three dates I still wasn't sure if I was in or out of luck. Rea Friede was from Turku, had moved to Helsinki for work. We had gone to Ekberg for coffee, out for dinner a couple of times, the movies and a photography exhibit, nothing more intimate than that. I had avoided talking about myself and concentrated on listening. It was a start.

Last time we said our goodbyes, I had promised to give her a call within the next couple of days. That was three days ago. The next couple of days were starting to run out.

After the death of his business partner Max – whose wife he had screwed on the couch in his office – Eli had been seeking out my company a lot more often. Maybe he felt guilty about the role he'd played in causing Max's death and endangering my life at the same time. If I had shown up at Max's boat a few minutes earlier, chances are good I'd have taken a bullet between the eyes.

Sometimes Eli suggested I join him for a round of golf. He'd been accepted as a member of a high-end golf club thanks to his father-in-law, who helped him skip the line. Or he'd ask me to the movies, or just show up at my doorstep without warning. It had been less than a week since I'd seen him last, and now I bumped into him at the community's center. I was there to meet Director Weiss, who'd been trying to coax me into taking over as activity director. I had just informed him I wasn't the right man for the job. Eli strolled into the room, perfectly at home, and plopped down casually on the spare chair.

"Hey, little bro."

"We'd have plenty of work for a man like you," Weiss said in a pleading tone, and turned to Eli for backup.

"Assignment not good enough for you?"

"Police work is too irregular for me to head up clubs."

"It's not as if we see you much around here as it is," Weiss said. "Working with the clubs would give you a good reason to spend more time here. You'd get to know the other members of the community." He raked a hand through his thinning hair. I felt like a lost lamb being shepherded back into the fold, delicately but firmly. If that didn't work, harsher measures would be brought to bear.

"I came by to take you out for a beer," Eli said.

Weiss furrowed his growing forehead at the interruption. He hadn't finished with me yet. "We'd also have use for your competence in security matters."

"I'll keep that in mind," I said as I rose. Eli hopped up, too.

My brother's Benz was parked on Malminkatu. It was the latest model and must have gone for a cool hundred grand. That's why it was so glaring that one of the taillights was shattered.

"I was coming back from lunch when some old guy backed into my taillight and said it was my fault. The little troll was about five two in his hat, jumping up and down and screaming like a banshee that it was my fault and he wanted payment in cash, because checks are a scam and credit cards are from the Devil. And guess what? I'm so insane I went and paid him €300 in repair costs for a tiny dent in his ancient piece of Jap shit, when I should have called the cops and made the old cunt pay me. Fixing the Benz is going to cost me at least a grand, not to mention the insurance points. Guess why I paid?"

"Because you're such a nice guy?"

"Because I imagined what it would look like if it read on the front page of the tabloids that a rich Jewish lawyer crashed his Benz and made an invalid vet shell out his last pennies to pay for it."

"I doubt he was a World War II vet. He'd have to be at least eighty-five. And the tabloids wouldn't have been interested, and it wouldn't have read Jewish lawyer." Then I remembered Oksanen's kike comment, and I wasn't so sure anymore.

"OK, so an old man's money. Not much better. The point is, I've started having some pretty weird thoughts lately. Does that mean I'm getting old?"

"What do you mean, getting?"

But Eli wasn't thrown by a jab from his little brother. I hadn't been able to get under his skin since we were teenagers. Back then he had flown into a rage when I borrowed his brand-new suede blazer and got mustard all over the front.

The second I opened my front door, Eli extended a hand, made a beeline for the fridge, latched onto a bottle of beer, and popped it open, completing the sequence of movements with a long swig.

"If anyone deserves a beer, I do. It's been a crazy day," Eli sighed. "I have a brilliant idea," he continued, when I collapsed on the sofa.

I didn't have to pretend not to care. I didn't.

"Silja and I are headed out to the cabin this weekend to get it ready for the summer. It's supposed to be warm this weekend. Why don't you and Rea come with us. We can sit around the bonfire all night…"

Eli and Silja's summer cabin wasn't a cabin; it was a massive wooden manor on the sea. And there was no need to get it ready for the summer. It was equipped for year-round use.

"No thanks."

"But you're coming to Seder, right? That's not up for discussion."

Seder was an important part of Pesach, which served as the basis for the Christian Easter. It's when Jews commemorate the release from bondage in Egypt with friends, relatives, and family.

"We can talk about that later."

"No, we can't. You automatically say no these days whenever I suggest something. What's wrong with wanting to spend more time with your little brother? We never know when this journey is going to come to an end, and then it will be too late."

Eli would have sounded more convincing if he hadn't been concentrating so intently on his beer and the game show on TV. I hadn't mentioned a thing about Rea to Eli, but I wasn't surprised he knew about us. Of course he knew his bachelor brother had been seen around town with a beautiful Jewish woman. That would have been as impossible to keep secret as the coastal artillery's live-round drills.

"I hope you're serious about that woman."

"I'm always serious at the beginning."

"Why don't you try being serious at the end, too, for once. I want to throw a proper bachelor party for you and a blowout wedding. Why don't you give your big brother and the community that little pleasure? Everyone's panting for confirmed bachelor Ariel Kafka's traditional wedding."

"So you want me to get married to please you and the rest of the community?"

"Two perfectly good reasons. At least don't hem and haw. Make your move as soon as it feels like it."

"Thanks for the advice."

"It's unfortunate that dating isn't a DVD you can fast forward. Or rewind, for that matter. Marriage has the same problem. Otherwise there are a few scenes I'd skip."

"Do you know a lawyer named Henry Silén, who disappeared a couple of months ago?"

"Everyone knows Henry. Did he turn up? Alive, I hope."

"No. What are people in the field saying about his disappearance?"

"Some say one thing, others say something else. He had a big list of investor clients, and the word on the street is that a lot of them lost their money and that's why it was wisest for him to disappear. Last two times he was in similar debacles he disappeared to the States for months."

"What debacles?"

"First time was over a dozen years ago. It had something to do with a major endowment from some foundation and investing the money. The endowment was donated about the same time the founder of the foundation died. The family members felt Silén had transferred money overseas that belonged to them."

"What happened in the end?"

"The endowment recipient, I don't remember who it was, came to an understanding with the claimants."

"What about the other case?"

"You should remember that one. It was about five years ago. He got sixteen months with no probation for aggravated fraud. A classic case. Bought worthless real estate with client money and when the money evaporated, he tried to say he'd just had a run of bad luck with investments. I was surprised Silén let himself make such a basic blunder. He's not stupid, but he's greedy. That can blur your judgment. This latest case is unfortunate in that these new investors are on the feistier side, motorcycle gangs and the like."

"What do you think happened?"

"You weren't dumb enough to give him your rubles to invest, were you?"

"What rubles? I don't have any rubles to invest."

"A methodical savings plan can work miracles. Well, not for you, maybe. I heard he had a house in Portugal. He's probably there."

"Without saying anything to his wife?"

"I can't say until I see the wife. Plenty of men have headed out to buy a pack of cigarettes and disappeared down that smooth road. The only one who knows what's going through a man's head is the man himself."

"There's also a rumor that he's been killed."

"I find that hard to believe. It's pretty rare to get your money back from a dead man. Is there a new development in the case, or why are you asking?"

I didn't answer, and Eli griped: "I forgot my little brother whose ass I used to wipe and diapers I used to change doesn't trust me. That's the way it's always been and always will be."

"You don't share information about your clients, either."

16

One of the most miserable sides to this job is waking up with a hangover at the crack of dawn to your boss calling and ordering you to take over a crime scene investigation. Eli and I had hung out at my place for a couple of rounds and then headed out to a local pub to continue. He'd wanted to treat me to a rare island malt. It was refined and expensive, so refined that it tempted me into indulging in an immoderate number of rounds, especially when Eli claimed to have caught a hint of something only a poet could accurately express. By the time we said goodnight, I was moderately inebriated as a result of all this immoderation.

So of course the phone woke me up immoderately early, in other words a quarter past six. It was Huovinen.

"Sorry for the early wake-up, but I want you to head out to Roihuvuori and assume responsibility for an investigation."

I was having a hard time focusing but managed to ask: "What's going on?"

"The bank manager you told me about yesterday has been killed."

"Halme?"

"Yes. There might well be a connection to your present investigation."

Halme dead, I thought. He was supposed to send me a list of the members of the Sacred Vault. That's as far as I got in my musings before my thoughts dissipated.

"The body was found in the terrain between Marjaniemi and Roihuvuori, near the allotment gardens. He was probably killed late last night."

I knew the area. A buddy of mine had owned a little cottage in the allotment gardens. It was like a suburb for Santa's elves. The cabins were teeny, tidy, and red. The garden gnomes looked like the inhabitants, the owners like curious tourists.

"Are you in any shape to go?" Huovinen asked, after noting the thickness in my voice.

"Eli and I had a few last night, that's all."

"Sounds like more than a few. Can you drive?"

"I wouldn't take the risk, and I don't have a car anyway."

"I'll have Simolin pick you up," Huovinen said.

"Thanks."

The thanks was sarcastic, but it was lost on Huovinen.

Simolin and I drove in silence against the traffic to eastern Helsinki. Once the ibuprofen kicked in, I was able to concentrate on Halme's death. I was sure it had to do with Laurén one way or another. I just couldn't figure out why Laurén would have killed Halme, unless he was afraid Halme was about to reveal something about him he didn't want made public.

"Where does Halme live?" I asked Simolin, certain that he already knew.

"Jollas."

"So he had some reason to be in Marjaniemi last night."

"Halme was supposed to give us that list of names," Simolin said. "Pretty strange coincidence that someone chose to get rid of him just now."

"It's not a coincidence."

I pictured the allotment garden area and had a thought. "Laurén is hiding out somewhere. An allotment garden cottage would be a good hiding place."

"Then Halme must have been lying to us. He knew how to get in touch with Laurén, maybe even knew where he is." Simolin's tone was disapproving. "But if the killer was Laurén and he's staying in a cottage, why would he have killed Halme right on his doorstep? He'd be risking getting caught."

"I don't think it was Laurén. Remember, Halme said he was going to make a few calls. Maybe he called the wrong person."

"No one kills just because they're about to be exposed as a member of the Vault."

"You're right, unless they'll also be exposed as Anteroinen's or Kivalo's killer."

We reached the spot where the body was found a little after seven. The directions led us from Tulisuontie onto a dirt road. After a drive of about a hundred yards, we reached a green metal side gate. It had a sign that read *Forest Gate.*

The morning gloom had brightened into a gray, windy spring day. The body was lying in a ditch, half-covered by a bush and dry underbrush. A pair of legs dressed in un-bank-manager-like jeans rose up to the edge of the ditch. I squatted down. The right cheek was pressed against the soil and crushed rock; the left was clearly visible. Sometimes death froze people in peculiar positions. Some dead people looked alarmed, some surprised, some drowsy. One eye might be open, the other closed, the mouth gaping. Generally people just looked like they had fallen asleep in the middle of dying. Halme looked thoughtful. Maybe it was because the rock under his cheek was pressing the corner of his eye up. The fact that the blood from the gunshot wound had continued the arch of his eyebrows might have added to the impression. It looked like a clumsy beautician had smudged makeup into his brows.

The crime scene investigators were there, along with the duty sergeant, Leimu from Takamäki's team.

"Shot at least twice with a .22," he said.

"Robbery?"

"Doesn't look like it. No phone, though. Wallet was there, driver's license in it. Made for an easy ID. Dog walker found him around 5:30."

Leimu handed me the wallet. In addition to the driver's license, it contained a little over two hundred euros, a credit card, some business cards, and a couple of parking tickets. Leimu jiggled the keys. They belonged to a Volvo.

"Any sign of the car? I doubt he came by bus if he had keys in his pocket."

"The closest cars are on Tulisuontie," Leimu said.

"Could you call in for the registration? We already know the make. Then you check the vicinity to find it. Or just try the key with any nearby Volvos."

Through the trees, I saw Vuorio's Benz pull up. He parked a good hundred yards away on the dirt road.

"Doesn't anyone else work at the medical examiner's anymore?" I asked, as he walked up.

"I could ask you the same question."

I left Vuorio to do what he did best and stepped aside. Simolin and Leimu followed me.

As I looked around, I had a flash of inspiration. I remembered a trick a crime scene investigator had taught me during an investigation of the murder of two Arabs at Linnunlaulu.

"Just a sec."

I rushed back over to the body and bent down to examine Halme's footwear. A pair of walking shoes with deep grooves. The grooves contained bits of the jagged gravel that covered the paths in the allotment garden.

Vuorio shot me an amused look. I returned to Simolin and Leimu. I addressed Leimu first: "Bring in more officers to cordon off the area and search the garden cottages. The dead man might have met an individual we're searching for in one of them. And I want you to take over the cottage searches," I said, lightly jabbing Simolin.

Simolin eyed the gardens stretching out beyond. "There are quite a few of them, a couple hundred at least."

"They're still empty this early in the year. If my memory serves me right, you're not allowed to move in until May Day. If someone is staying in one, it will be obvious… or wait one more sec."

I had Laurén's wife's number in my phone. Judging by how chipper she sounded, she'd been awake before I called. I'd pictured her as the sleeping-in type. After identifying myself, I asked: "Do you know which one of your ex-husband's friends has a cottage at the Marjaniemi allotment gardens?"

"What makes you think any of them do?" she said. "None, as far as I know."

"There was an old picture in your photo album from a garden party. There was a white cottage with green trim in the background. Whose was it?"

"Oh, that. Now I remember. That was in Marjaniemi. It was before Mandi."

"Whose cottage is it?"

"Sotamaa's, or I guess it was his parents' back then. I only went there once… what about it?"

I thanked her and hung up. "Laurén's college buddy has a cottage here. He might be holed up there… wait one more sec."

My next call hit the bullseye. This time, there was no doubt Sotamaa had been roused when the phone rang.

"Your family has a cottage at Marjaniemi. I want the address and number."

"What the hell… calling in the middle of the night… what cottage —"

"Stop yanking my chain," I snapped. "Give me the address. And if you call Laurén to warn him after we hang up I'm going to make sure you face charges of hindering an investigation."

Sotamaa frittered away a few seconds as he weighed the situation.

"Puolukkatie 177. How the fuck did you guys find out… can we make a deal that you won't tell —"

I covered the phone's mic and whispered to Simolin: "Puolukkatie 177." He understood me the first time and went and grabbed a police patrol to accompany him.

I continued grilling Sotamaa: "Why don't we agree here and now you're going to tell me what's going on. You've been misleading the police. You might not believe it, but that's a bad thing."

"Come on, it can't be a crime to put a roof over an old pal's head… you guys weren't looking for him back then… and I still don't know what he's suspected of, so I can't be guilty of doing anything."

He was right, but there was no point letting him know that.

"Besides, I'm pretty sure I told you I like cops as much as I like having ticks on my balls. For me, they represent the machinery of violence. Not ticks, cops."

It was a new slur, and I gave Sotamaa some points for that. Usually we had to listen to the same old tired jokes and unimaginative insults.

"If you really want to know, he's suspected of a couple of murders. As a tiny cog in the machinery of violence, it's my job to investigate such things." I was exaggerating, but I figured a fearful, guilt-ridden Sotamaa would be more talkative than a self-confident cop-hater. "If he commits another one, part of the burden will fall on your shoulders."

Sotamaa couldn't think of anything else to say than "Fucking fucking fuck."

"What was the reason he gave you for needing a place to stay? He has an apartment in Töölö."

"Because some crazy bastard from his drug-using days was after him."

"When did he move into the cottage?"

"About a week ago."

"What else did he tell you?"

"Nothing. I gave him the keys and told him not to show his face outside, because you're only supposed to stay in the cottages during the summer."

"Does the name Kai Halme mean anything to you?"

"Of course I know Kaitsu. Old Daybreak crew."

"Who else knew where Laurén was staying?"

"No one, as far as I know. I didn't tell anyone, that's for sure. When I brought him to the cottage, some custodian saw us, but… Now I have a couple of questions of my own to ask —"

I left Sotamaa in the throes of a healthy uncertainty and ended the call.

"The gate's locked," Simolin said. I glanced over and saw the fence was crowned with four-inch finials. One of those in the wrong place would feel highly unpleasant.

Sergeant Leimu followed the fence and called out: "There aren't any spikes on the pedestrian gate."

The smaller gate was a good ten yards from the one intended for vehicles. It was low enough that scrambling over it was no problem.

"This is Muuraintie. There's got to be a map of the area somewhere near the main gate," Simolin said, as we marched toward the eastern edge of the gardens.

"If we only knew where that was," Sergeant Leimu said.

The gravel crackled under our feet. A sky-blue cottage, apple trees, and decorative ironwork gate; Mustikkatie, a pale-yellow cottage, and a red toolshed. Bushes and flowerbeds and a couple of apple trees.

Sergeant Leimu noticed it first: "Puolukkatie."

"147. The next one is 149. The numbers increase as they move northwards," Simolin announced.

After walking almost a hundred yards, I recognized the cottage from the photo album. The number 177 on the doorjamb helped. The cottage was more decrepit than its neighbors. The unpainted wooden gate was as weathered as an old barn. The felt roof looked like it was sagging. The windows were trimmed in decorative light-green woodwork. Sotamaa hadn't seemed like much of a handyman; he probably didn't even own a power drill. He had blithely allowed the cottage tended with such care by the previous generation to fall apart.

As I moved closer, I noted the dark curtains pulled across the windows.

"Who are we looking for, the killer?" Leimu asked. He'd been resolutely silent up until now.

"I think Halme came to see whoever is staying in the cottage."

"Is he dangerous?" one of the police officers asked, reaching for his Glock.

"I don't think so. You guys go around and approach the rear from the neighboring lot. He might try to escape out the back."

The police officers headed off to look around the back. I gave them two minutes. Then I opened the gate; the hinges squeaked, begging to be oiled. There was no movement anywhere, or any sign that there was anyone inside the cottage.

I paused to listen outside the door before knocking loudly. Out of the corner of my eye, I could see the policemen approaching in the cover of the trees.

"Laurén! Come out, it's Ariel."

Using my first name, which carried symbolic value for Laurén, was a conscious tactic. I knocked again, but still nothing. I tried the door. It was unlocked, and cracked open.

"Laurén, I want to talk to you," I announced, stepping in. I sniffed the air like a proper bloodhound. It smelled of damp rag rug, coffee, and butane.

The cottage was tiny, so I hit the rear wall almost immediately. To the right there was a combined living room and bedroom, with a green sleeping bag bunched up on the bed. A small dresser butted up against the foot of the bed; an armchair covered with a green blanket stood in the corner. The decor consisted of a cheap color print on the wall, peasants making hay. The sun-drenched work was clearly a copy of some famous oil painting. As I glanced at the floor, I discovered the source of the butane smell: an old-fashioned heater next to the wall. I turned left toward something resembling a kitchenette. The table there had a coffee mug on it, along with a pint of low-fat milk, a package of margarine, a hunk of cheese, a couple of bananas, an opened strawberry yogurt, and a loaf of rye bread with a slice cut out of it. I tested the kettle. It was still hot.

We had interrupted Laurén's modest breakfast. He fled from us a hungry man.

I silently cursed Sotamaa. My threats hadn't frightened him enough. He had warned his buddy after all.

I peered out into the yard from the rear window. I saw a pair of policemen crouched down behind a berry bush, weapons raised. I turned right back to Simolin, who had followed at my heels.

"Have them send over more men and any mobile patrols to look for Laurén. He just left, and he was in a hurry. We've got to bring him in. If he didn't kill Halme, he knows who did."

I returned to the forest gate; one of the patrols had found Halme's car in a church parking lot a few hundred yards away. It was a late-model Volvo wagon. The officer handed me the keys. Maybe he was afraid of contaminating the scene.

I circled around to the passenger side to search the glove compartment. I wasn't expecting to find anything interesting, so I wasn't disappointed. In the back seat there was a car blanket, nothing else. I opened the armrest and found a blue diary with Halme's name printed on the cover: a gift from the Helsinki Police Officers'

Union. I flipped through the pages until an underlined note struck my eye. Above the line was a familiar name: Arto Kalliola, Deputy National Police Commissioner, Ministry of the Interior.

17

"Strange," Huovinen said, upon hearing my report of the morning's events. He looked tired and agitated. It hadn't been the best spring for him. His Estonian-born wife had been diagnosed with breast cancer, and they'd had some water damage at home. The pipes in their newish house had frozen while they were on vacation, and when they returned, the bathroom and front hall had been inundated.

"Halme is exactly the sort of guy you can picture Kalliola knowing. He scrounges for visits to places like Halme's company. They usually bring the diary as a gift for the host. Hundreds of them are in circulation."

"I know. The real question is why Halme underlined Kalliola's name. I'm betting he either had been in contact or was planning on contacting him, and right after we met with him."

"Maybe he just called Kalliola out of curiosity to tell him you two met, and to ask what sort of guy you are."

"Could be. What about Laurén?"

"It's not him. If he killed Halme, I'm pretty sure he wouldn't have hung around the cottage waiting for the police to show up. He ran at the last minute. I believe either the owner of the cottage or the ex-wife warned him about us."

Huovinen switched to an easier topic. "What other alternatives do we have open to us?"

"It could theoretically have something to do with Halme's own life, but when you consider the time frame and the place he was killed, we have to assume his death is related to the rest of the case."

"Which is getting messier and messier by the day."

"Simolin will have finished a preliminary gutting of the student rosters by our meeting this afternoon. After that, we'll have a net in the water we can slowly start tightening. We can go through the students one by one."

"Pretty hard to imagine that boarding at Daybreak would have given rise to numerous avengers, and that they'd be killing each other on top of that. At least Laurén's motives and actions are somewhat understandable. And that crime reporter from *Ilta-Sanomat*. What if you contacted him to find out what Laurén's intentions are? They clearly have some sort of agreement."

I promised to call, even though I knew it would be pointless. Moisio was your typical hardheaded reporter who believed source protection meant he wasn't even obliged to divulge the brand of tax-free shop deodorant he used.

"This afternoon in the conference room," Huovinen reminded me on his way out of my office.

*

Fresh butter-eye buns had been provided with the conference room coffee in honor of the presence of the National Bureau of Investigation. Our visitors were Lieutenant Tommi Hult and Sergeant Pekka Nikinoja. I'd met both of them before, but I couldn't claim to know them. Generally any meetings with the NBI were held at their premises in Vantaa, which said something about our relative status in the hierarchy. Those lower on the totem pole visited those higher up, not the other way around. This time, however, Hult had suggested we meet in Pasila. Maybe they were tired of gazing out at farms and fields and wanted a breather in town. Huovinen, Simolin, and Stenman were also present.

"How do you propose dividing up the work?" Hult asked Huovinen.

"We're not proposing that yet, but it looks like we have two, perhaps three murders that have occurred around Finland, along with one in Spain, and one likely perpetrator who is on the loose. We decided it was only proper to inform the NBI." Huovinen had chosen to play his hand carefully. No point shoving the case down their throats. That just aroused resistance.

"I'm still not particularly convinced, based on what I've heard," Hult said.

"Convinced of what?" I asked.

"That your conclusions are accurate, that we're dealing with a serial killer. This Laurén worked at a funeral home contracted to the medical examiner's office and could have heard these confidential details one way or another. The fact that he applied for such work with a background like his indicates a fascination with death. Coupled with the schizophrenia, that explains a lot."

"Nothing is as certain as death, but we feel that under the circumstances it's better to play it safe. We're fine handling the investigation on our own."

Nikinoja chimed in: "Is it true that Laurén has been in contact with you several times?"

"Yes. Called me twice and sent me two letters. He promised to contact me again and explain more when the time is right."

"So we can say that ultimately he wants to be caught. Why would he talk to you about his crimes, anyway? Doesn't he already have a reporter he tells everything to?"

"Seems to. Moisio from *Ilta-Sanomat.* He's received confidential information in advance on two occasions." Per Huovinen's request, I had called the reporter again and suggested another meeting, but he hadn't seen any use for one. Said the wishes of the police force and my stance had been made clear during our first meeting. "But 'wants' isn't the right word. He knows he'll be caught and has accepted that. It's part of the plan, whatever that is. We could use your help, because you could have your men in the provinces look into the backgrounds of the deceased. We can do it, too, but it's more efficient to do it in person than by telephone."

"Simolin, why don't you share with everyone what you discovered about the incident in Spain?" Huovinen said.

Simolin was flustered by the attention and concentrated on his notes to get past the embarrassment. "With the help of our local lead, I managed to get my hands

156

on the preliminary investigative material, which is of course, in Spanish. I also received Interpol's request for police assistance that was made to Finland at the time. I haven't had time to have it all translated yet, but the main points have been read to me. I can also read some Spanish myself…" Simolin's embarrassment was deepened by this admission, but he plugged on tenaciously. "The victim was Veijo Kivalo, former headmaster of the Daybreak Academy. He was driving home from Malaga in the early evening when the car was somehow ordered to stop and forced onto a side road. The incident bears many of the hallmarks of a normal car robbery, which are relatively frequent there; what's rarer is for the victim to be killed, let alone burned alive. According to the coroner, the victim was alive when the car ignited or was ignited. He had smoke particles in his lungs. The victim was quite social, an active participant in the Finnish community on the Costa del Sol. He had many friends and no known enemies. He was a widower and lived alone in Fuengirola."

"I could go to Spain to do some digging around. Seventy-seven in the shade is perfect investigative weather," Nikinoja joked. He was thirty years old, tops, but nearly bald.

"It's not the paradise it used to be, unless you're a Russian mafioso or Baltic crook," Hult said. "I read an article in one of the tabloids that said the majority of the seaside real estate there is in the hands of Eastern European criminals. And then of course you have the Finnish drug kingpins hiding out there."

Nikinoja ignored his lecture: "That doesn't change the weather."

The intervening commentary threw Simolin. After scanning his papers for a moment, he continued: "The perpetrator or perpetrators didn't leave any traces, nor were any eyewitnesses found. The only clue was that Kivalo had spoken via telephone with one of his local Finnish friends in Spain and indicated that he was going to meet a Finn that day. He hadn't revealed a name or anything else about this compatriot, even whether it was a man or a woman."

"Did they search Kivalo's apartment?" Huovinen asked.

"The Spanish police considered it a clear case of robbery–homicide, and as a result, the home search was superficial. They didn't find anything out of the ordinary. Kivalo owned the apartment, so they left everything as it was. His nearest relative, in this case his daughter, was informed. She went to Spain and retrieved anything of personal interest before putting the place up for sale, which she did as soon as the estate was settled. The daughter lives in Minnesota, but I got hold of her there last night. She remembers finding a letter among her father's belongings that had been mailed from Finland a couple of months earlier. It didn't have the sender's name, but based on the postmark, it was mailed from Helsinki. It stuck in her mind because all it read was *Ye serpents, ye generation of vipers, how can ye escape the damnation of hell?* I checked the precise wording from the Bible. It's from the Gospel of Saint Matthew, chapter 23, verse 33."

I interrupted Simolin with a glance. "This same Bible passage was written on the back of the body discovered in Laurén's apartment. There was additionally a verse from Psalms 91, the one that goes something like this: *He shall give his angels charge over thee, to keep thee in all thy ways...*" I turned to Simolin to help me out.

"*They shall bear thee up in their hands, lest thou dash thy foot against a stone. Thou shalt tread upon the lion and adder: the young lion and the dragon shalt thou trample under feet...*"

"So we have three bodies, Anteroinen, Kivalo, and Sandberg, who all have links to the Daybreak Academy. Kivalo the headmaster, Anteroinen the maintenance man, and Sandberg, the CFO of the B. E. Kajasto Foundation. In accordance with a change in the foundation's governing principles, the 30-plus million markkas and other property Kajasto left the foundation, including real estate in Helsinki, was to be dedicated primarily to developing Daybreak. Sandberg handled the transfer of the endowment on the foundation's behalf. And then Attorney Henry Silén invested at least twenty million markkas of foundation money in various mutual funds. Laurén studied at Daybreak. It can't be a coincidence. Laurén has to have been involved in the murders somehow; maybe he's the murderer, or at least one of them. Laurén spoke of five evils. If Silén is the fourth and is already dead, that means there's one more to go. So we have to look for the fifth among the same cohort, which is pretty large, or what, Simolin?" I said, tossing the ball back to him.

Simolin had reviewed the student rosters he had received from Daybreak. "Pretty big. If we limit our search to three years, there are still about a hundred students plus Daybreak staff. There were around forty people in Laurén's class, seven of whom are dead. That's a surprisingly high number for such a young group."

Hult roused himself. "How did they die?"

"Three by their own hand, one in a car accident, one drowned, one from health complications, one was stabbed to death."

I pointed out that the students were spread all over the country, as were the suspected crimes, and there was no way our little team could investigate everything effectively enough.

"I think we're done here; we're going into overtime," Hult said. "Why don't we proceed by you prepping a proposal containing everything concrete you want us to handle. I'll fast-track it through."

Huovinen clearly had no use for the bureaucracy this entailed, but was forced to capitulate. "Ari is probably the best person to take care of that."

Huovinen left to see the visitors out. I stayed in the conference room. There was still coffee in the thermos and butter-eye rolls in the basket. I could tell by the look on Simolin's face that he still had something he was bursting to tell.

"There's one interesting name in the student roster," he said, a little hesitantly. "When you think about the theft of the bodies and how it was done…"

"Lay it on me."

"One of the students in Laurén's class was Esa-Pekka Vuorio."

"So? It's a common enough name."

"Yes, but Esa-Pekka Vuorio happens to be medical examiner Esko Vuorio's little brother. I checked it out. There's no doubt."

Simolin's revelation silenced me.

"What does he do, this Esa-Pekka?" Stenman asked.

"Nothing. He's dead. He's one of the ones who killed himself. Was a successful and respected internist who killed himself at his summer cabin."

Stenman turned to me. "What do you think?"

"Based on what we saw on the surveillance tapes, it would make a lot of sense that someone on the inside helped Laurén with the body."

"If Vuorio helped Laurén steal the body, is it possible he was otherwise involved?" Simolin said, still with an odd timidity. The notion was clearly repugnant to him. Simolin was fond of Vuorio, just as I was. Vuorio had been a mentor of sorts to him. Vuorio would ponder things at a crime scene with Simolin that he typically only communicated post-autopsy.

"Such as?"

"What if Roosa Nevala's death wasn't a suicide after all?"

"So Laurén would have killed her and Vuorio helped with a cover-up?"

"That was the first thing to cross my mind."

I knew what I had to do, even though I didn't want to. "If – at this point, everything is still speculation – if Vuorio helped Laurén, you'd think it would have something to do with him knowing Vuorio's little brother.

Which in turn implies revenge, in other words that he's helping Laurén get back at someone who he feels drove his brother to suicide."

"Särkijärvi?" Simolin suggested.

"Presumably. It's a shitty situation, but all we can do is ask him directly."

I was on my way out the door when I remembered something: "Find out if Heikki Moisio is related to Moisio the reporter. Heikki Moisio was a former Daybreaker too."

Simolin hurried off to his office. Immediately afterward, Huovinen stuck his head in the room and crooked his finger at me. I followed him into the corridor and closed the door behind me.

He only said one word: "Oksanen."

"What about him?"

"He was ordered over at a breathalyzer checkpoint in Koivuhaka and fled the scene at speeds approaching 120 miles per hour. His car was found near his home with the doors open. He's at home but refuses to open the door. Three patrols are there. Get over there and make sure he doesn't ruin his chances permanently. Handle it as gracefully as you can."

I had driven Oksanen home to Puistola plenty of times, so I knew where he lived. After his divorce, he'd used an inheritance to buy a modest postwar house for the big garage on the lot. Without his nagging wife around to put the brakes on his favorite pastime, he'd popped it into high gear and let it fly.

"Absolutely."

18

When I got to Oksanen's place, two of the patrols were already gone, or at least they had moved their vehicles further away. The police knew it was a colleague's home and were doing their best to avoid arousing the neighbors' attention. The presence of three police cars would have brought the first reporter to the scene in under an hour.

I found an officer lounging casually in a metal lawn chair. "Are you sure he's in there?"

"Yeah. We just talked to him."

"What did he say?"

"Fuck off! I don't mean you; that's what he said." The cop, who had been hardened by house calls, appeared amused.

I wasn't. "So he's drunk?"

"At least 1.5 percent. Can tell by the way he's slurring. I'm guessing he's playing for time so he can claim he didn't start drinking till he got home. It's a good strategy, tried and tested in court."

"Did he claim someone else was driving the car?"

"We didn't get that far in our uplifting conversation. He's listening to music now."

I circled around to the junk-strewn backyard, knocking over a front fender that was leaning against the wall as I rounded the corner. I didn't recognize the brand, but it was emblazoned with an ad for an auto supply business. It clattered down onto a stack of rims with an ear-splitting screech. Without making any more noise, I picked my way through Oksanen's wrecking yard to the living-room window. The officer was right. I could hear the music clearly: 'Riders on the Storm'. I was fond of The Doors myself.

I heard Oksanen's drunken voice stumbling as it tried to keep time with Jim Morrison. He more or less caught up by the time the chorus started.

I knocked on the window. No response.

I knocked again so hard I was afraid I'd break the glass.

Oksanen's head and a hand holding a bottle appeared next to the window. He glared down at me, took a swig of beer, then closed the blinds without saying a word.

"Oksanen!"

No response.

I pulled out my phone and called Oksanen's number. I got a prerecorded message: *The number you are trying to reach is out of service.*

I went back to the front yard. A large garage and a small shed, its wall decorated with a half-dozen old-fashioned chromed hubcaps, stood at the far end. The lot was bordered by a dense, overgrown hedge. Everything pointed to the fact that there wasn't a woman on the premises; just a man who was into cars.

"You're right, he's listening to music: The Doors."

"At least he has good taste," the officer said. He glanced at his partner and continued: "It doesn't make any sense to have three patrols hanging out here wasting time. Either we're going in or we're leaving. Is he dangerous?"

"I don't think so."

"But as a police officer, he has his police firearm, right?"

"I suppose."

"What if you tell him through the mail slot that either he comes out or we're bringing the SWAT team in. They'll crash in with the doorjamb around their necks. But that means half a dozen reporters and photographers here before you can spit."

"There's no mail slot. He has a mailbox."

"So shout through the window or the door." The police officer was right. Threats might do the trick.

I climbed three steps up to the front door and pounded on it. I could faintly hear the strains of 'Light My Fire'.

I pounded again. A moment later the music faded.

"What the fuck are you knocking out there for? I'm gonna call the cops."

"They're already out here with me. They're thinking you'd better come out or they'll bring the SWAT team in."

Now I could hear Oksanen's voice right next to the door. "What the fuck for? Can't I listen to music in my own house?"

"You were driving drunk and fled the scene over the

165

speed limit. That's bad enough on its own. If we have to call in the SWAT team, you know what the consequences will be."

"Drunk and speeding. Is that what they're saying? I disagree, disagree a whole hell of a lot."

"And now you're disobeying police orders."

"In the first place, I wasn't driving. I was sitting in the passenger seat. This other guy was driving."

"So come out with this guy so we can clear things up."

"He already left. He didn't hang around, even though I asked him to. He was hitchhiking and I picked him up… somewhere. No idea who he was, but he knew how to drive."

"Then come out and clear things up alone."

"And thirdly, how can I be disobeying police orders when I didn't even know there are police officers out there? I thought my asshole of a neighbor was at the door again, bitching about the noise."

"So who am I, then?"

"No idea. Besides, I'd rather go lay down now. I'm really fucking tired."

"No. We're going to clear this up now."

Oksanen paused for a moment to think. I waited, intrigued.

"Let's assume you're Detective Kafka, which actually disqualifies you," he began. "You've already demonstrated a hostile attitude towards me. I want to talk to someone else. But this is just an assumption, because I don't know who you really are."

"Stop clowning around. I'm not investigating this case. The patrol that followed you is going to do the reporting. You want me to have the officer come over to talk with you?"

Oksanen forgot that he didn't know who I was. "Tell me one thing, Ari. What do you have against me? Be honest."

"Nothing."

"Stop screwing with me. You think I haven't noticed? You're always laughing at me behind my back… I know the score. I'm not going to let some Middle Eastern leatherworker or rug seller piss in my eye."

I felt a pang of conscience. It was true that I had joked with others about Oksanen, or more precisely his motor racing.

"I've never laughed at you, just your cars. It annoys me because it gets in the way of your work. And that's the truth."

"No, it doesn't," Oksanen said, his voice surprisingly docile.

"Yes, it does. I counted that you were abroad four times last year at police rallies, twice while you were on the clock —"

"With permission from the ministry," Oksanen interjected.

"— plus you spend hours online and on the phone looking for some turbocharger or other thingamajig for your car and then you drive halfway across Finland to pick it up."

"I have your thingamajig swinging between my legs."

I had to struggle to keep from bursting into laughter. "Time's up. The boys from the precinct want to call in the SWAT team."

"What if I come out? Then what?"

"You'll be questioned on suspicion of driving under the influence and disobeying orders."

"I just told you, I didn't do either. In theory, I couldn't have even heard the police, because I was playing '60s classics so loudly and I didn't touch any booze until I got home. My car was being driven by that infamous criminal we all know so well, aka an unidentified suspect. You think it'll work?"

"You can always try."

"The assholes won't believe me, even though this time it's the truth. That means I'll get the boot."

"Probably, but you could reapply for your job once the mandatory probationary period is over. You'll definitely get the boot if you don't come out and clear things up."

"They believed that former MP. Couldn't prove she'd been driving drunk. The law needs to treat everyone equally. Right?"

Based on what he was saying, Oksanen was a lot more inebriated than I'd realized.

"What about that woman's letter accusing me of all sorts of stuff?"

"What about it?"

"Are you going to be investigating it?"

"No, but someone will."

The door opened, and Oksanen stepped out. A bottle of beer dangled from his hand. His eyes were glazed.

"Would you believe me if I told you I've always done my work to the best of my abilities? I'm actually a pretty good cop, if I do say so myself."

I didn't say anything, but I didn't deny it. He plopped down onto the steps. I sat down next to him.

"I'd rather have a bullet in the brain from a drug dealer than get caught for a ridiculous little thing like this."

"Who wouldn't?"

"So what's the story? You gonna cuff me?"

"You go in and tell your version of what happened. Then you get to go home."

"What about work?"

"You're on sick leave." I eyed Oksanen. "Although you don't look like you're having back trouble."

"The pain isn't visible on the surface. What about afterward?"

"Bigger wigs than me will make that call. The fact of the matter is, I don't harbor any ill will toward you. If you spent less time on your cars while you're supposed to be working, you'd be exactly the sort of guy I need."

"You think I don't know Simolin's your favorite?" Oksanen said, staring at the flagstone step between his feet.

"He's a good detective who focuses on his work 100 percent. We investigate the most serious crimes imaginable, manslaughter and murder. It's not work you can approach half-heartedly. We have mothers desperate for us to find their child's killer, kids desperate for us

169

to find their father's killer. Those people's lives are at stake, their peace of mind. If you were my subordinate, say, at an appliance repair shop, I might be a little more lenient about your leisure pursuits."

"I'd be fixing fridges and vacuum cleaners."

"Exactly. You follow me?"

"I'm not that stupid, of course I follow. It's true I've been fooling around with cars a little too much, but I've done my best when I've had time."

The officer walked up to us. "We need to get going. The control center is starting to put pressure on us. Three patrols have been stuck here for an hour already. That means they're not out there doing their patrolling."

I steered the guy aside. "Do you mind if I take it from here? There's no problem anymore."

"We have to administer a breathalyzer."

I went back over to Oksanen. "They have to administer a breathalyzer."

"They gotta do what they gotta do."

He blew 1.8 percent.

I promised the officer I'd bring Oksanen down to HQ and have someone question him.

"You're a lieutenant, so I trust you, but he's your headache now."

I held out my hand, and the officer shook it.

I went back over to the steps where Oksanen was sitting, lowered a hand to his shoulder and tried to act as natural as possible. "Go get your coat. I'm on duty today. I can give you a ride home after you've been questioned."

Out of the blue, Oksanen covered his face with his hands and started bawling. It took me a second to realize he was crying. Snot and tears were oozing out between his fingers.

He wiped his face and looked at me. "Police work is the best thing to ever happen to me. If I get the boot, I might as well shoot myself through the head… for a little while there I was considering it. Ari, help me. Everyone respects you and will listen to you. Please speak up for me."

It's not often you see eyes as pleading as Oksanen's. It was the look of a whipped dog pleading for mercy.

"Whatever; I'm already headed downhill, might as well pull out the stops. Everything has gone to shit since Sinikka left."

"OK, but let's go."

"What's wrong with women? When I'd try to get close to her, she'd say, do you always gotta paw at me – she's from Savo. When I'd ease off, she thought I was cheating on her." Oksanen turned to look at me. "You probably don't know what I'm talking about. You're single, or a bachelor or whatever. Tell me why you can't get a woman, even though you're a good-looking, foreign-looking guy…"

"I wish I knew."

"Arja would drop into your lap like a ripe fruit if you put in the tiniest bit of effort."

"I think it's time for us to get going," I said, and stood.

"You promise to put in a good word for me?"

"I already said I would."

"Shake on it." Oksanen shoved his hand into mine. I had to shake it. "And sorry about that Jewish thing. I was being stupid. Please please please forget I said it."

I promised I would, even though I knew I couldn't.

19

Less than an hour later, I was at Vuorio's place in Tammisalo. His brick '60s house would have been considered high-fashion vintage; I could picture it being auctioned alongside Chanel jackets, Cartier jewelry, and Hermès bags.

I'd decided Vuorio had guessed the reason for my visit, because he hadn't asked any questions when I'd called and asked to meet him that night.

The original hardwood front door opened, revealing Vuorio in a loose, lightweight sweater, soft burgundy sweats, and checked slippers. His red scalp gleamed through his sparse, silvery hair.

"Come in. Looks like the end of a long day."

"Long enough."

Vuorio steered me into the living room. I sat down on a comfortable-looking leather sofa. It looked like an Italian or Danish classic, and felt like one, too.

"I could use one of these at my place," I said, patting it.

"When we moved here, my wife got the best money could buy. She had a sense of style like no one else."

A portrait by the same artist who had done the oil painting in Vuorio's office hung over the mantel, only this one was bigger. The woman seemed to be keeping an eye on the room with her slightly imperious gaze.

"This was her dream home, so I gave her free rein. Can I get you a drink?"

"No, thanks."

"My wife isn't to blame for those; I put them up after she passed away," Vuorio continued, nodding at the end wall, which was adorned with the head of a spiral-horned antelope, African spears, a shield, a leopard skin, and a collection of hunting knives. "I shot the antelope myself; the leopard skin I bought from a local. My wife never would have let me display tacky dust-gatherers, as she would have put it."

I couldn't decide how to begin, even though I'd spent the entire drive trying to figure that out.

Vuorio broke the silence. "Ask away; that's why you're here."

"I'd like to ask you about your brother."

"Esa-Pekka. How did you find out about him so quickly? Simolin, I presume?"

"Yes."

"He's good at that sort of thing... Esa-Pekka was over ten years my junior. By the time he started high school, I was at med school. He was gifted, much more gifted than I am. He should have been allowed to live..." Vuorio turned to look at the picture of his wife, another dead loved one. "Do you know why he killed himself?"

"Your brother? Because of what happened at Daybreak."

"What Särkijärvi did to him left a scar that never healed. I thought he had finally gotten over it when he graduated and got married... Guess what the worst thing about it was? I was so wrapped up in my work that I didn't pay attention to what was going on with him. There were years when I only saw him at Christmas. If I'd have been the big brother I should have been, I'm sure he would have talked to me about it. I could have done something. I swear I would have; I would have cut Särkijärvi's balls off; it doesn't take me more than the flick of a wrist," Vuorio said, slamming his fist against the armrest of his chair.

"When did you find out?"

"Not until after he started med school. I heard about it from Laurén. I brought it up with Esa-Pekka, but he refused to talk about it, even though I could tell he was suffering."

"So you admit that you know Laurén?"

Vuorio glanced my way and grunted. "Why wouldn't I? He was in my brother's class at Daybreak."

"Do you admit the rest, too?"

"What rest? Are you suspecting me of helping Laurén steal the body or conceal evidence?"

"Wouldn't you, if you were in my shoes?"

"No doubt. How shall I put this... I respect you as an investigator, and I don't want you wasting your time barking up the wrong tree. Roosa Nevala wasn't killed; she committed suicide. She left Laurén a letter giving him permission to use her body for his purposes and burn it. You can have a clear conscience that I know nothing that would be of use in investigating the Marjaniemi murder, or any other murder, for that fact. And investigating anything else isn't your job. I will only say this to you off the record. I'd like to retire with no fuss."

"I can imagine you helping Laurén by, say, leaving the door open, but I can't imagine you helping him carry the body up to the apartment. But someone did. One alternative is Moisio, the reporter who did the story on the disappearance of the body. What do you think?"

"Perfectly feasible, based on what I know about the man. For him, the news justifies the means."

"So what are Laurén's intentions, if he isn't planning on murdering anyone?"

"To expose what happened at Daybreak. He's using the media as a weapon, not a gun or a knife."

I started getting impatient. "But the Marjaniemi case has to relate to Laurén one way or another."

"I don't know any more about it than you do; less, even."

"Maybe someone doesn't want what happened at Daybreak to come out yet?"

"Särkijärvi might be many things, but he's not a killer. And if that were the case, Laurén is the one he should have killed, not Halme."

"Maybe he followed Halme to try to get to Laurén but got caught and killed him."

"That might make some sense if he weren't in Brussels," Vuorio remarked. He seemed irritatingly blasé for a man

176

who had just admitted to having aided the bodysnatcher. On the other hand, he was aware of the position he was in.

"When was the last time you met or talked with Laurén?"

"About a week ago. He called to arrange a few matters. I told him I didn't want to be involved in anything else from that point on."

"He didn't call today, after he escaped from us in Marjaniemi?" I asked, studying Vuorio's face.

"No."

"And you didn't call him? Someone warned him."

"It wasn't me. Do you want to check my phone for the calls I made and received today?"

"No, not for the moment."

"There's something else I want to make clear. That conversation with Laurén a week ago had nothing to do with Halme."

"But you knew Halme?"

"I met him at one of Esa-Pekka's parties in college. I had no trouble remembering him, even after all those years. I was just as surprised as you were when I ID'd him this morning. He was shot with a .22, by the way – a rifle, I'd bet. Judging by the spot I found one of the shells at, the first shot was fired from a distance, over ten yards away and slightly concealed, which also indicates a rifle. The second was fired from a few dozen inches away to make sure he was dead. Those guns often have silencers these days. All you hear is the click of the firing pin."

"You didn't think any of this was worth telling me?" I said, trying for sarcasm.

"I was too surprised. And what could I have said? I met him twenty years ago at some shindig?"

"You didn't suspect Laurén for a single moment?"

"No. They were friends. And Laurén would never shoot anyone. He hates guns."

I stood and looked around. I could see a bookshelf through the open door to the study. "You have a lot of guns?"

"Half a dozen. A big-game rifle, a .308 for moose hunting, a bird gun, a couple of shotguns, and a .22. I have permits for all of them." Amazingly, Vuorio had the restraint to keep from adding the question *You don't think Halme was killed with one of my guns, do you?* "The guns are in a locked case. I can show them to you if you'd like."

"No need. What do you mean by he's using the media, not guns?"

"He has contacts in the press —"

"Moisio at *Ilta-Sanomat*, we know. So he means to go public with what happened at Daybreak. That was over twenty years ago. Who cares anymore?"

"Oh, people will care, if it's offered in a pretty enough package."

"Are the body's theft and the funeral pyre part of that package?"

Vuorio considered his words carefully: "One could put it that way."

I stood and stared at him. He had already taken shelter in the sanctuary of his memories, and wasn't the least bit perturbed.

"You're taking one hell of a risk. I have to talk to Huovinen about this."

"Of course you do," Vuorio said nonchalantly. "By the way, would you be interested in joining us for a goose hunt towards the end of the summer? It's a gentleman's sport."

"I'm not a gentleman."

I hadn't had many days like that, even though the work of a detective is more colorful than that of your average accountant. I'd headed out that morning with a wicked hangover to investigate the murder of the bank manager I had met the previous day, wrangled with the NBI, and negotiated the end of a siege between the police and a drunken subordinate who had run away from them. To cap it off, I'd discovered that a medical examiner I'd known and trusted for years had been implicated in the theft of a body. All I wanted was a shower and my own bed.

On the way home, I picked up some tandoori from the local Indian joint. The aroma tickled my nose as I walked down the street; I could already taste the spicy chicken in my mouth. Chase it down with a cold beer... I'd already forgotten the pain of the hangover the way a mother forgets the agonies of childbirth and is raring for a new round before she knows it.

"Ariel!"

I turned in the direction of the shout to see a hand waving from a light-colored car I had just walked past. We were no more than a couple hundred yards from my place. I moved closer, because the voice sounded familiar.

The man in the car reached across to the passenger side, and the light from the streetlamp struck his face. Despite the baseball cap I immediately recognized him. He looked a lot older than he did in the photographs. It was Laurén. He had rolled down the window far enough for me to hear him, no more.

"I didn't kill Halme."

I'd left my firearm at HQ and had no interest in using force. Besides, I was exhausted and had my dinner dangling from one hand. So I decided to listen.

"Open the door and I'll hop in."

"No."

I saw the sticker of a car rental agency on the side window. A description of the vehicle wouldn't be much use.

"How did you hear about Halme's death? Who warned you?"

"It doesn't matter."

"Yes, it does, because the only ones who knew about it were the police and the killer."

"It doesn't matter, believe me," Laurén said obstinately.

"So what happened in Marjaniemi?" I asked, leaning in until my face was nearly up against the window.

"Halme called to tell me you'd been in touch and wanted a list of members of the Sacred Vault. He also wanted to know why you were looking for me."

"And why is that?" I asked.

Laurén looked surprised. His surprise surprised me. "Because of the theft and the funeral pyre."

"Nothing else?"

"What do you mean?"

"In my view, and not just mine, your letters gave the impression you know who killed Anteroinen, assuming you didn't do it yourself, and that more bodies are on the way."

"I don't know who killed Anteroinen, and I don't care. It was a good deed. The way he'd lived his life meant an end like that was inevitable."

"Headmaster Kivalo was also killed."

"I can't say I'm very sad about that either. And I didn't mean to threaten anyone. I just repeated what it says in the Bible: God will wreak his vengeance upon evildoers."

"Did you need to steal a body for that? Well, that's a matter of opinion. Anteroinen molested children; Kivalo was worried about Daybreak's reputation and turned a blind eye... what about Särkijärvi?"

The name made Laurén start. It was like he had slammed on the brakes.

"The Bible requires us to forgive our enemies. I love that book, but I can never forgive... if you knew how many souls that man has destroyed..." Laurén's movements became compulsive, as if he were no longer in control of them. I saw him clench his fists.

"Let's get back to Halme. So you met him last night. What time did he leave?"

It took a moment before Laurén was aware of my question.

"He never showed. He was supposed to come around eleven, but I never saw him."

"He didn't call to tell you he couldn't make it?"

"No. I tried to call him, but he didn't answer."

"Who knew where you were hiding out? Except Sotamaa."

"No one." The tiny delay in Laurén's reply told me he was lying.

"Someone had to know, otherwise the killer wouldn't have known to expect Halme."

"Maybe he and Halme came together." Laurén's reply indicated that he might be crazy, but he wasn't stupid.

"What reason would anyone have to kill Halme?"

"Maybe he ran into some nutcase. It might have something to do with me, or it might be completely unrelated. Maybe he slept with the wrong man's wife. He's been that way ever since he was young. I've lied to his girlfriends for him dozens of times. The killer might be one of the women or husbands he screwed over."

Laurén's words threw me. Jealousy had been the farthest motive from my mind.

"Give me names if you have any."

"Say, the current headmaster at Daybreak, Hätönen. He's a former student. He went into education, and Halme and I used to run into him at parties during college. He had a fiancée; I think her name was Kristiina. Halme hit on her, and that was it for Hätönen and Kristiina."

"Was he also a member of the Sacred Vault?"

"Hätönen? Not on your life. He wasn't involved in anything that would have put his relationship with Daybreak's administration in jeopardy. The Vault was way too radical; the administration didn't look kindly on it."

Laurén clearly didn't care for people of Hätönen's ilk. But when it came down to it, who did?

I steered the conversation back on track. "A husband who had been cheated on would otherwise fit the bill, but not now, because we're talking about the location and timing of the crime. Halme was killed as soon as he got in touch with you."

"There's nothing more I can do for you." Laurén looked past me, not in distance, but in time.

"I'm becoming more and more interested in knowing who the members of the Sacred Vault were. You can help me with that."

"I only know the ones who were in it at the same time I was. The Vault is much older."

"Let's start with them."

"Now isn't the time. I just wanted to tell you it wasn't me. You can count on that. I've made a vow to God to stick to the truth."

I glanced at the meal in my hand. I lifted it up. "I want to eat this while it's still warm."

"Indian?"

"Tandoori chicken. Why don't you come into HQ tomorrow and we can go through the whole mess again?"

"No, not yet."

"When, then? There's an APB out on you."

"So keep searching. I'll come in as soon as my labors are finished. There is much to be done, but the laborers are few."

"You're not planning on avenging yourself on Särkijärvi in any way, are you?"

"I never said that. What I said was I wouldn't kill him… and I'm not doing it for myself, but for a lot of other people…" Laurén's voice started quivering. "Tonto, my best friend from Daybreak, is lying in a coma… at least three people have killed themselves. Isn't that enough of a reason?"

"I'll have to tell my superiors that we spoke."

"Go ahead. Good night, and God bless."

"Wait a minute. Someone has killed three former Daybreak employees and now one student, a member of the Vault. If it's not you, you might be next in line."

"For he shall give his angels charge over thee, to keep thee in all thy ways. Thou shalt not be afraid for the terror by night; nor for the arrow that flieth by day." Laurén rolled up the window and drove off.

I wrote down the license plate, even though I doubted it would do any good. The car would turn up somewhere, the driver wouldn't. But I still called the plate in and asked all patrols to keep an eye out while going about their duties.

At home, I opened up the plastic takeout container and set the naan out on a plate next it. The food had cooled so much that the aroma's pungency had already dissipated.

The worst of it was, I wasn't the least bit hungry anymore.

20

Simolin was like a well-trained bird dog. At a command, he took off after the scent, sniffing through the woods and alder brush and returning only when he could drop the bird he'd pointed at his master's feet. Then he'd lunge off in pursuit of fresh prey.

I could instantly tell from the look on his face that he'd made another discovery. Nevertheless, he calmly seated himself across the table from me. I was in the canteen, with the salad of the day and a glass of kvass in front of me. The busiest lunch rush had passed, and there was no one in earshot.

"Well?"

"I think I figured out why that reporter named Moisio from *Ilta-Sanomat* is so well-informed. According to the student roster, a Heikki Ilmari Moisio was one year ahead of Laurén. After Daybreak, he got into law school and became a lawyer, first in Oulu and then Helsinki. Not quite two years ago he was stabbed to death in a building entryway in Kallio. The assailant was never caught."

"Is he related to the reporter?"

"Big brother. Four years' difference. The dad was a widower who owned a fur farm. He was religious, but the boys had gotten feral without a mother around. The older one had a conviction for narcotics possession, and the younger one was a troublemaker in school. Dad sent the older one to Daybreak Academy to break him in. The younger one was sent off to live with relatives in southern Finland; when the old man died, he inherited the farm, which was in debt."

"Where did you get this information?"

"I called a fellow Native American enthusiast who lives in the same town. The Moisio brothers have a reputation there. My guess is *Ilta-Sanomat* Moisio got to know Laurén through his older brother. Which is also why Laurén picked him as his trusted reporter. Maybe the younger Moisio sees himself as being part of a joint revenge plan."

"The older Moisio brother's death doesn't necessarily have anything to do with the case. It's not as if he's the first person to ever be stabbed in Kallio."

"There's no evidence, of course, but at least it gives a plausible explanation for the collaboration between Laurén and Moisio."

Simolin's hunch was probably more accurate than mine.

"Good work. Find out who investigated the Moisio stabbing and talk to them. I'll be out of the office for a couple of hours, and my phone might be on silent. Leave a message if there's anything urgent."

*

I watched the woman's hands as she set down the coffee cup in front of me. I could see they were shaking. I thought I caught the sound of cup clinking against saucer.

Saimi Vartiainen was a petite, uptight woman, and not just psychologically, but physically uptight, too. She was like a mummy that had been wrapped so securely that her rib bones creaked.

"I stand by what I wrote," she said, seating herself at the table. At the same time, she pushed a plate of chocolate cookies in my direction. I took one out of politeness.

Ms. Vartiainen's living room was surprisingly youthful and breezy for an old woman's home. The furnishings in her Oulunkylä apartment were few, and tastefully chosen. The building was on an arterial; I distinctly heard the sound of buses rumble past. No wedding picture or high-school graduation photos of children or grandchildren. All signs pointed to Ms. Vartiainen being an old maid. I took a bite of the cookie and, since I had been raised to mind my manners, swallowed it before I said: "I don't doubt it. I just want to make sure you know what you're in for. I'm not trying to intimidate you, either, but if we decide to launch an investigation, we'll have to interrogate you officially – or we won't, but our colleagues from Espoo will."

"So it's not a clear-cut case?"

"Is anything ever? There's also another if. If the prosecutor decides to press charges, the matter will go to court. In all likelihood, the case will be of interest to the media, which means reporters will want to interview you, too."

"That sure sounds like intimidation to me," she said dryly. "What's your relationship to him again?"

"I'm his boss."

"Of course." Ms. Vartiainen managed to load the two words with an incredible amount of implication.

"Isn't it natural that, as his superior, I want to be the first to hear what my subordinate is being accused of? Don't worry, there's no way I can make this go away, even if I wanted to."

"Do you want to?" She looked at me, her neck rigid.

"No. You promised to provide us with more evidence."

She passed an unsealed manila envelope lying on the table across to me. "I've kept a record of all of the visits Detective Oksanen and that other man from the Ministry of the Interior made to our company. You can have the diaries where I made the original notations if you want. In addition, I always made myself a note on those occasions when I was made privy to what they requested from Mr. Berg, for instance if they asked the company to sponsor a foreign trip to some police rally competition. There are at least three such instances. The company sponsored those trips to the tune of €3,000. Or when they asked for spare parts for cars. Of course I didn't hear anything close to everything, but after each visit Mr. Berg generally told me to handle the matter. To inform the sales floor about the discounts and the accounting department about funds that needed to be paid to the rally club's account. I'm sure you'll find evidence of the transfers in both the company's and the club's bank records."

"Have you informed Mr. Berg regarding your request we open an investigation?"

"Of course not, but I believe he will approve of – or at least understand – my decision. He mentioned on several occasions how awkward he found the situation."

"Didn't you ever question him as to why he continued sponsoring the club?"

"It's not an administrative assistant's place to ask such questions."

I looked over Ms. Vartiainen's head. Three colorful oil paintings hung on the opposite wall. One, a portrait of a young woman, I recognized as the work of Unto Pusa, and another as that of Sam Vanni. The painter of the third was unknown to me. The arrangement was relatively mundane, but the work had personality.

Ms. Vartiainen noticed my gaze. "Do you like those paintings?"

"They're superb. Pusa and Vanni; who's the third?"

"Gösta Diehl. I inherited it from my father. Are you fond of modern art?"

I admitted I was. But as interested as I was in postwar modernism, I didn't pause to discuss the topic, nor could I have.

"Of course, we'll have to question Mr. Berg as a witness. He'll be subpoenaed to provide testimony in court. If he thought things were awkward before, this will be a whole new ball of wax." I instantly regretted my words. I had instinctively taken sides, not necessarily Oksanen's, but that of a fellow police officer.

Ms. Vartiainen paid no attention, though. It seemed as if she were considering the matter from this vantage point for the first time.

"Won't my testimony suffice?"

"Unfortunately, the allegations are of such a serious nature that we'll need all possible supporting evidence. You mentioned that Oksanen was blackmailing your boss somehow. How would that even be possible?"

"That's what I assumed, because Mr. Berg was clearly dismayed by Detective Oksanen's requests but still didn't refuse them."

"Is that all?"

"Oksanen also spoke in hints, as if he knew something unpleasant about the company or could find out if he wanted to, thanks to his status as a police officer."

"How did the other man who accompanied Oksanen behave?"

"What was his name again? He had a round face and a loud voice. I had no problem hearing him through the door."

"Arto Kalliola. He's the deputy national police commissioner, works at the Ministry of the Interior."

"A big fish, then. He left the begging to Oksanen and just sat there quietly, but when the deals had been cut, he'd blossom into a real glad-hander. Pat everyone on the back and be so convivial."

I had suspected something of the sort. Kalliola was an old fox; Oksanen was just the errand boy.

"He's not going to get off scot-free, is he?" Ms. Vartiainen asked, as if she could read my thoughts.

"If Oksanen is investigated, Kalliola will be investigated, too."

Ms. Vartiainen started pouring more coffee, but I politely refused. One chocolate cookie was enough, too.

"Do you have any idea what Oksanen could have been using to blackmail or threaten Mr. Berg?"

Ms. Vartiainen shook her head; not a single strand of her gray hair moved. They were as disciplined as their mistress.

"Have you already told Detective Oksanen and this... Kalliola about me?"

"Not about you, but about the allegations."

"How did they react?"

"It's probably best if I don't comment."

"If the case goes to court, what will happen to them?"

"Depends on if they're convicted."

"And if they are?"

"They'll probably be fired... but I don't think that makes much difference anymore, at least in Oksanen's case."

"How so?" Ms. Vartiainen asked doubtfully.

I knew I was in murky waters, but for some reason I felt the need to defend Oksanen. I didn't feel like kicking the guy when he was down. He was like a family member you'll defend against outsiders even if you'd knock his block off when among your own. "Detective Oksanen was so upset by the allegations of bribery that he took sick leave and started drinking. Got caught drinking and driving at a police checkpoint. A DUI alone will be enough cause for firing."

I didn't expect such a strong reaction. Ms. Vartiainen looked horrified and nearly jumped out of her chair.

"Excuse me…" To have something to do, she collected the empty coffee cups and carried them unsteadily to the kitchen sink. She lingered in the kitchen for at least a couple of minutes, clinking the dishes. When she returned, the mummy-like tautness was gone, as if the brittle wrapping cloths had disintegrated. She looked much softer.

"Sometimes it seems as if God punishes wrongdoers on our behalf. I believe one punishment is enough for Oksanen." She fingered her spectacles nervously as she said: "What if I told you I wanted to retract the allegations against Detective Oksanen?"

My phone vibrated, indicating an incoming message. I glanced at it: *Call!!! It's important. Seija Haapala.*

Laurén's ex-wife's text message and its three exclamation points made me momentarily lose my train of thought. I had to focus to get back on track.

"Then I'd discuss the matter with my superior and we'd consider how to proceed. It won't necessarily change anything. If we determine that in our view Oksanen has committed a crime, we have a duty to investigate."

"I'm not saying that Detective Oksanen didn't do wrong, but it seems as if he has already received his punishment. So let's call the whole thing off, no matter what you may think of me."

Ms. Vartiainen took her notes from the table and shredded them. "No copy of these exists."

"I didn't tell you about Detective Oksanen because I wanted to pressure you either way," I said. But the truth was, I had manipulated Ms. Vartiainen, whether I wanted to admit it or not.

"If I thought you had, I'd be demanding Detective Oksanen's punishment even more vehemently. I consider myself a good judge of character, and I can see you're an honest man."

"I hope so."

I didn't know which I meant myself: that I hoped I was honest, or that I hoped she believed I was.

I called Seija Haapala the moment I got outside. "You tried to reach me."

"Is it true Kai Halme was murdered?"

"Where did you hear that?"

"Ola called and told me. Was it Reka?"

"We don't know who did it. Were you the one who warned him we were coming?"

"Absolutely not. I'm the last one he'd tell where he's hiding out."

"Maybe you heard from Sotamaa. You two are on good terms."

"What's that supposed to mean?"

"Are you telling me you aren't?"

"Not as good as someone might think, reading between the lines of what you just said." The realization came like a bolt out of the blue, the way they usually do. I remembered Laurén's bitterness when he talked about Halme's intrigues with women.

"You and Halme had an affair, too."

I heard a deep sigh. "That was over fifteen years ago. It was as short as it was hot."

I continued taking potshots to see if my luck would hold out. "Is Mandi Halme's daughter?"

"You're letting your imagination get the better of you. Halme knew how to make a woman feel good; we had our fun. Everything would have been just fine, but Ola found out by accident and had to go and spill the beans. In any case, Reka is Mandi's father and that's that. No need to start coming up with far-fetched theories."

"Are you afraid your ex-husband killed Halme out of jealousy?"

"It occurred to me, when I heard where the killing took place. I don't get why Reka would have done it, though. It's been so long he would have had no shortage of better opportunities if he wanted to kill Kai. The more I think about it, the crazier the idea sounds."

"Does the name Ossi Hätönen mean anything to you?"

"No. Who's he?"

"The current headmaster at the Daybreak Academy. Attended at the same time as your ex-husband. Reka clearly had something against him."

"Then I know who he is. Hätönen showed up once by chance when Särkivaara or whatever that teacher's name was —"

"Särkijärvi."

"— when Särkijärvi was fondling Reka in the music room. Reka asked Hätönen to tell the headmaster what he'd seen. Hätönen chickened out and claimed he didn't see anything. Reka hated him."

"What about Heikki Moisio? Does the name say anything to you? He's *Ilta-Sanomat* reporter Jyri Moisio's brother and another former boarding student from Daybreak."

"I've never heard of him, but his brother, that reporter, wouldn't stop calling me about a year ago."

"Why?"

"He asked me to let Reka know he wanted to get in touch with him."

"A year ago?"

"At least. Something occurred to me: since you guys are so set on finding former members of the Sacred Vault, I'm assuming you know the Daybreak Academy is celebrating its centennial this spring, and alumni from around the world will be attending. Former members of the Vault will definitely be participating. Reka got an invitation, too."

21

I had to admit that I would have been up the creek if Simolin had stayed in Canada contemplating Native Americans. The case Laurén had kicked off was swelling to such dimensions that we were drowning in leads. Luckily Simolin was an organized man. He didn't need any convoluted Excel spreadsheets to put the pieces we'd gathered into place and concentrate on what was relevant. I'd asked him to prepare an interim summary of the investigation; the big picture was easier to grasp when you intermittently reviewed what information you had. Getting a handle on this disintegrating case was like trying to get a grip on wet toilet paper. It was also time to re-evaluate the overall tack we had taken.

Simolin browsed through his notebook, where drawings of Native American headdresses and other regalia appeared among the notes. My personal preference was for coloring in squares and doodling jagged lightning bolts.

"We have five homicides, all of which have taken place within a three-year period. Kivalo was the first to be killed, then Sandberg, then Anteroinen, then Moisio, and last of all Halme. On top of that, Silén is missing. Five unsolved homicides. That's a lot in such a short period, especially if we assume that it's the same perp. Is it possible someone could have murdered five people they knew without anyone being able to connect the cases…"

"That's hard to believe; you have a point," Stenman conceded.

"I don't believe it, either, even if the killer would have had the fact going for him that the crimes took place all over Finland and abroad. I don't think it's the same perp in every case. I met the investigator from the Moisio stabbing and don't believe it's part of the same series. Moisio used drugs, amphetamines and cocaine, and a small amount of cocaine was found on the body. The investigator thinks the stabbing was drug-related. The word was the attorney had crossed swords with his client, a big-time drug dealer. The crook suspected Moisio ratted him out to the cops about a money-laundering operation so the police wouldn't look too closely at his own affairs. And the MO was so different than in the other four cases. On the other hand, Anteroinen's criminal activity might also have been the motive for his murder."

"Do you think Anteroinen could have been using drugs… or selling them? That might be a link between the cases," Stenman pondered.

"Moisio lived in Helsinki; Anteroinen lived in Kouvola. The attorney would have had no trouble getting his fixes without Anteroinen. Anteroinen's case also diverges from the others in two more ways. Number one: Anteroinen's is the only case where revenge dating from his time at

Daybreak makes sense as a motive. He molested students, so it's easy enough to imagine that one of them, or even a loved one of a suicide victim, would have wanted revenge."

"Why hasn't anyone killed Särkijärvi?" I asked.

"He's been living abroad."

"That didn't protect Kivalo."

"Kivalo was married; same goes for Sandberg. Both had kids. No one has even hinted that they had anything to do with molesting the boys. And Silén's disappearance more likely has to do with his own business affairs than Daybreak."

"So we still don't have much to work with."

"What was the second factor that set Anteroinen apart from the other cases?" Stenman asked.

"Of all the victims, Anteroinen was the only one who was working class. All the rest were educated."

"What could that have to do with the case?" I asked.

"Anteroinen was a big guy, violent. Maybe someone used him as a bodyguard or to intimidate…" Simolin was clearly thinking out loud. "Or maybe Anteroinen was hired by someone to kill Kivalo or Sandberg, after which he was killed to keep him quiet or when he started blackmailing whoever commissioned the hits."

"We're sliding into speculation. Which of the homicides do you think are the handiwork of the same perp?"

"Sandberg and Kivalo. One was burned, the other drowned."

I noticed that I had scribbled in my notebook a lightning bolt over a three-tiered pyramid. "Fine. Sandberg and

Kivalo were both in leadership positions at Daybreak; in other words, they were both responsible for the fact that Anteroinen and Särkijärvi weren't called to account for their actions. Both of them were more concerned about the academy's reputation. Is that enough of a motive?"

"Maybe."

Stenman gave her two cents: "And Halme was killed because he knew something about the perpetrator."

"Why now, though?"

I remembered Laurén and the cottage at Marjaniemi. "There are two alternatives to what happened at the allotment gardens. Halme either met Laurén at the cottage and only at that point learned something dangerous. Or, as Laurén himself claims, Halme tried to see him, which was enough to spook the murderer."

We had come full circle again. The killer had to be someone from Laurén's or Halme's inner circle, someone who knew about the cottage and the meeting.

"According to Laurén's daughter, Sotamaa has the hots for her mother. Halme had an affair with the former Mrs. Laurén, too. Maybe Sotamaa was afraid Halme would steal her a second time. And he knew about the cottage. That would mean the motive wouldn't have anything to do with the other cases."

My idea didn't generate any support, which was fine; I didn't believe it myself.

"I'm still more of a mind that Halme found something out, for instance who killed Kivalo or Sandberg, or why. Knowing the reason can be just as dangerous as knowing who did it."

Halme had made a positive impression on me. He'd felt guilty that he hadn't told anyone about what his friend had been forced to suffer. I was sure he wouldn't want to give someone away who had simply avenged injustices he'd experienced, and I said so to Simolin and Stenman.

"You might be right," Simolin conceded, jotting down something in his notebook. "But the opposite might be true, too: maybe he had something to hide. Maybe he was complicit in the abuse of his classmate, helped Särkijärvi in hope of some benefit, and Laurén lured him into a trap."

"Halme and Laurén have been friends this whole time. I doubt that would be the case if Halme had helped Särkijärvi or Anteroinen. But go on."

"The technical investigation of Halme's car didn't reveal anything new. They found dark-blue fibers on the passenger seat, but without anything to compare them to, they're no good. The shooter probably drove to the scene. After all, he was carrying a rifle; transporting it would have been difficult without a car."

"Unless it was in a guitar case," I said, thinking of Sotamaa.

"Vuorio is the only person related to the case who has a rifle permit. And his .22 is equipped with a silencer. But it's the wrong make. He has a Sako; Halme was shot with a Russian Toz. There are thousands of them in Finland."

"What do we do with Vuorio?" I asked. I had told both of them about the house call I had paid to the medical examiner.

Simolin wasn't the type to throw the first stone. "I believe he helped Laurén by leaving the door to the morgue open or moving the corpse outside, but that's all."

"There's no point wasting energy on that now. We can't prove anything. He's a sly old fox," I said.

"What did Huovinen say?" Stenman asked.

"Let it be for now. We'll take another look at it once we've apprehended Laurén. Besides, I'm starting to think we set off in the wrong direction. We believed Laurén was involved in the killings and was planning more; he certainly wrote as if he knew more. But it's possible he simply heard about them, like many other former students of the academy. He's just come up with an interpretation compatible with his worldview and is talking about God's vengeance now."

"This would be easy if you always knew the right direction to take from the get-go," Simolin said.

"Daybreak turns 100 a week from now. Former students have been invited to the celebration. I'm going to meet the headmaster today. You guys concentrate on the Halme case. A quick run through his phone logs, but before that I want you to go to his home and his office. Look through his notes and his diary, talk to his secretary and wife." I turned to Stenman. "What did our new bishop know about the Sacred Vault, by the way?"

"A few names. Laurén, Halme, Moisio, and that professor at Oxford. Thought it was juvenile foolishness. Knew Laurén had had psychological problems, and admitted Laurén had phoned him and called him a traitor after he'd been made bishop. Didn't know Sandberg or Silén.

Remembered Kivalo and Anteroinen, of course, but didn't know they were dead. But the second I asked about pedophiles, he got cagey. Maybe bishops are supposed to be cagey, but he claimed he didn't want to spread malicious rumors."

My phone rang. I could tell the call was from *Ilta-Sanomat*: I'd come to recognize the first few digits. The two last digits were the same as Moisio's. I rejected the call and said: "I think that was Moisio. It looks like he's doing a story on Laurén's plans."

"I'm guessing he's not going to tell us if he learns something?" Simolin said.

"I'm guessing you're right."

"If I were Laurén, I'd cause some sort of uproar at Daybreak's centennial."

Simolin's remark was like being whacked over the head with a log. How had I missed such an obvious connection? The celebration was a week away. If Laurén was planning public revenge, he wouldn't have a better opportunity. And the reporter and his photographer would have seats reserved in the front row, of course.

"I think I'll call Moisio back after all."

We met on neutral territory, the cafeteria at the Eläintarha gas station.

"I was a little impolite last time we spoke," Moisio observed, with a humble look. His right hand was stroking his expensive watch.

"You wanted to talk about something?" I said.

"I thought it might be my turn to offer something. When it comes down to it, we're on the same side."

"And whose side would that be?"

"The public's. Source protection wasn't created as a prop for the media so we'd be able to shoot innocent people from the bushes, but so we'd continue to learn about injustices in the future, too. Sounds pretentious, but that's the way it is."

"What are you proposing?"

"You know how I've been in touch with Laurén? He has given me stories, and I can assure you he's working for a good cause."

I had heard this before. It was almost verbatim what Vuorio had said to calm me down.

"I'd sleep better if I knew what that cause was."

"He wants to use the media to bring Daybreak's deep dark secrets into the light. That's all he cares about. You don't have anything against that, do you? That I expose individuals who sexually abused students?"

"Expose whatever you want, as long as you don't aid and abet criminal activity. Laurén is being sought on suspicion of having committed a serious crime, and if you know where he's staying, that's exactly what you're doing."

"I don't know. Can I ask you something? You don't think Laurén killed Halme, do you?"

"No comment."

"If that's what you think, you're way off base. My brother went to school with Laurén, and I've known the guy for years. If anyone despises violence, it's him."

"It doesn't sound like it."

"He might go a little overboard in his letters and stuff, but that's more a stylistic conceit. The Bible is chock-full of crimes and violent threats, too."

"Did you know Halme?" I asked.

"I met him a couple times at my brother's parties. He had a lot of enemies, mostly cuckolded husbands," Moisio said, with a wry smile.

"What about your brother? Who killed him?"

The reporter's expression cooled a few degrees. "I'm still waiting for the police to figure that out."

"Is Laurén planning on organizing some sort of upset at Daybreak's centennial celebration?"

"How would I know?" Moisio said brusquely. He was clearly less than thrilled by the question. Evidently he feared for his scoop.

"I guess we'll be seeing each other there," I said.

22

Luckily we didn't have to drive ninety-odd miles to see Headmaster Hätönen. He was attending a two-day seminar right across the bay in Espoo, so he and I agreed to meet when it broke for lunch. I brought Stenman along with me.

It's hard to imagine a less inspiring site for a seminar than a dismal hotel complex located between an industrial park and the freeway, and yet the surroundings had done nothing to dampen Headmaster Ossi Hätönen's aura of energy. He bustled in swinging a black satchel. He was somewhere between forty and fifty, with short bristly hair. The overall effect was one of an irritable badger.

He gave me a superficial handshake but took his time with Stenman, then immediately dictated the conditions of our meeting: "Twenty minutes max."

"Let's get right down to it, then," I said. We were in a quiet corner of the lobby, and I lowered my notebook and pen to the table. "We're looking for your former student, Reijo Laurén, on suspicion of criminal activity."

"You mean the Academy's former student, not mine," Hätönen interjected. "To be frank, I've been perplexed by your inquiries and what you think you'll find. Those matters are ancient history, and it would be best to forget them."

"We suspect that Laurén's deeds and potential future deeds reach back to long-past events."

"What has he done, then?"

"That's confidential information as defined in police investigation law."

"You received the student rosters you requested; what else do you want?"

"Back in the day, an association called the Sacred Vault existed at the academy. The members were students. What do you know about it?"

"Not much, because it was a secret society, and they weren't allowed to talk about it with outsiders. I guess some of the boys were fascinated by it, in the same way forbidden fruit is fascinating. Downright childish, to be honest. But the Vault ended back in the late '80s."

"We want the names of the members," Stenman said.

"Little lady, I'd be more than happy to tell you if I knew. Aside from Laurén, the only one I know is our new bishop, Kaltio, but you've already been in touch with him. These days he views the Vault with amusement more than anything else."

Word travels fast, I thought.

"Who else?"

"Moisio, the attorney, he was on the Academy's board of directors for a couple of years. But he's already dead. I think that's about it —"

206

"What about bank manager Kai Halme?" Stenman asked.

"Oh yes, and him. He attended our last student reunion, five years ago."

"He was in your class, wasn't he?" I said.

Hätönen grew grimmer. "I meant that was the last time I saw him."

"Were you aware he was shot two days ago?"

"No, I had no idea. Who did it?"

"We're looking for the killer. We have some indications that it might have been a former student of Daybreak."

"Hundreds of students have come through Daybreak's doors. I still find it hard to believe —"

"I heard there was bad blood between yourself and Halme due to a broken-off engagement."

"He was a skirt-chaser and seduced any woman in sight given half a chance," Hätönen said, lips tightening.

"Including your fiancée?"

"Yes. Since then I've come to think of it as a lucky break. I learned what sort of woman she was before it was too late." Hätönen tried to produce a smile and failed miserably.

"Does the name Leo Anteroinen say anything? Or Lars Sandberg?" I asked.

"I believe you already asked about Anteroinen. I don't know what's true and what's gossip, so I prefer not to comment. He worked for us for some time under the previous headmaster. Apparently he was forced to resign due to various allegations."

"Didn't your predecessor Headmaster Kivalo tell you anything about it?"

"Why would he have? Those unpleasant events were already two decades old by that point. No memoranda on the subject exist, so everything is just talk – and as you well know, talk has a way of getting distorted over the years."

"Were you in contact with Headmaster Kivalo after he retired?"

"A few times. Of course, he also attended several student events. I was very sad to hear what happened to him. He enjoyed living in Spain so much."

"Did you ever meet him there?"

"In Spain? No. Wrong direction for me. I prefer Lapland."

Stenman picked up the ball: "Other members of the staff were also mixed up in these 'unpleasant events.'"

"Really? I hadn't heard that. I'm all ears."

"Didn't you witness an incident of sexual abuse?"

"Absolutely not. Apparently you've heard the kinds of rumors I try to avoid perpetuating."

Arguing was pointless, so I moved on. Hätönen was already glancing at his watch. "Daybreak turns 100 in a week. Are you planning a big celebration?"

"You could say so. We have a lot to celebrate."

"Who will be attending?"

"Present and former students, the leadership of the Church of the Redemption, several prominent church figures all the way from the US. Two local MPs have promised to attend. There will also be some higher-ups from the Department of Education, and then of course the Minister of Education is coming. He has agreed to speak."

"What about former teacher and social worker Vesa Särkijärvi?"

"He's another former member of our Daybreak community of whom we're particularly proud. He holds high office in the EU these days. He has also promised to speak."

"So you have his phone number. I'll go ahead and take it," I said.

Despite Hätönen's apparent reluctance, he couldn't think of a reason to refuse. He pulled up the number from his contacts list and then stood, sternly tapping his watch. "Time flies. I have to get going."

We watched him head for the restaurant, where a throng had already gathered at the door. I could almost see the wake he left behind him in the air.

"Slimeball," Stenman said, once Hätönen was out of earshot. I agreed. I had no trouble picturing him behaving exactly the way Laurén had claimed, denying having witnessed any abuse. The code of silence.

"I wonder if we shouldn't have a word with His Holiness Bishop Johan I," I mused.

"Wouldn't Särkijärvi make more sense? If he thinks he's a target, he might be more amenable to talking than the others."

"Sure. But he's not in Finland yet."

"Ari!"

The cry came from behind us. When I turned to look, I saw Rea approaching. She was wearing a black skirt, gray blazer, and mid-heel pumps, and her hair was up. I'd never seen her dressed for work before. It suited her; she looked efficient. I would have hired her on the spot.

She glanced at Stenman. "What are you —"

"Here for work. What about you?"

"An incredibly dull seminar. When you go through the trouble of coming to such an uninspiring place, the least you can expect is for the seminar to be interesting. Who were you here to see?"

"It has to do with the case I've been telling you about. We were asking about a few names."

I noticed Rea and Stenman eyeing each other.

"It must be quite the case, since you've already canceled on me twice because of it. You don't know what you missed out on," Rea said and smiled. She had a beautiful smile and suggestive eyes. I'd caught myself wondering one day what could be wrong with her, since she'd never been married. She did have a couple of long-term relationships behind her. Her most recent boyfriend had been German.

"I'm sorry," I said. "Sergeant Arja Stenman; Arja is my subordinate. Rea Friede."

They shook hands.

"I see you haven't found the right title for me yet," Rea said, still smiling. "I have to get going if I'm going to eat before the tedium continues."

"I'll call you tonight," I promised in a panic.

"Don't make promises you can't keep." Rea excused herself with a wave and made for the restaurant. If I wasn't imagining it, she was exaggerating the rock of her hips.

"Nice-looking woman," Stenman remarked a moment later. "Are you two dating?"

"Feeling things out."

"Is she Jewish?"

"Yes."

"Does it matter?"

"No, not to me, but I guess it doesn't hurt either. At least not in the minds of the Jewish community."

Stenman's query gave me the opportunity to get up to speed on her status. All I knew was that she had divorced her entrepreneur husband when he got caught selling fraudulent invoices. She had two children approaching adolescence.

"What about yourself? Are you dating? You don't have to answer."

"No. I think I've set the bar a little too high. And kids scare men off."

I didn't dare go any further.

Just as we were climbing into the car, a text message arrived from Huovinen: *Can you meet at 4?* I tapped out an affirmative response.

"Any news about Jari?" Stenman asked, after we had driven for a bit.

"No. His sick leave lasts another week."

"The divorce was hard on him."

"You may be right."

"It's funny," Stenman said, smoothly changing lanes. "Even though he's not a superstar, he fills a funny gap in our team. I don't know how else to put it."

I thought about Stenman's words and had to admit she

was right. I didn't know myself what Oksanen's particular competence consisted of, but there was something there.

I managed to reach Särkijärvi in Brussels before my meeting with Huovinen. According to his secretary, he'd been running from meeting to meeting. He seemed busy now, too.

"Kafka, was that the name?" he asked.

"Yes. I'm looking for an individual named Reijo Laurén. Can you help me?"

"Absolutely not. Why would you make that assumption?"

"But you do know him?"

"If it's the same Reijo Laurén. One of my former students was a Laurén, but that was over twenty years ago."

"It's the same individual. We learned he has a grudge against you and have come to the conclusion that he might have threatened you."

"Perhaps, but I wouldn't take it seriously. He suffers from psychological problems. What does that have to do with the police? What he needs is treatment."

"We're searching for him as part of an investigation involving the deaths of two former Daybreak Academy employees: the headmaster, Kivalo, and Leo Anteroinen, who was the maintenance man."

"Yes? I'm not sure how I can help you."

"You're scheduled to attend the academy's centennial, and we suspect Laurén is planning some sort of ambush at the party."

"Ambush?"

"According to him, you sexually abused him and other children during your time at Daybreak."

Särkijärvi's laugh was forced. "As I said, he has serious psychological problems. That's why I haven't wanted to involve the police… and still don't."

"When was the last time he was in touch with you?"

"About a month ago. If I can be candid, he suffers from obsession and delusions. He's been treated for acute psychosis. Unfortunately, I have to go. I'm expected at a committee meeting and as chair, I can't be late. If I were you, I'd take what he says with a grain of salt. Analyzing it is a job for a psychologist, not a detective."

I'd been expecting Huovinen to have company, but I was still surprised. He was at the table in our little break area, chatting away blithely with Oksanen over coffee.

"The prodigal son has returned, and his sins have been forgiven," Huovinen said.

I stood there, literally gaping.

"Sit down and I'll explain."

I took a seat next to Huovinen.

"We received a photo from the Vantaa Police yesterday, taken by a traffic enforcement camera on Ring Road III. They sent it to us because the car caught speeding was registered to one of our personnel. In other words, it's Jari's car."

I wondered why Huovinen still seemed to be in a good mood.

"But according to the photograph, it was someone else driving the vehicle."

"Who?"

Oksanen jumped in. "The guy I was telling you about. Who was nice enough to give me a ride home from the bar when I'd had one too many."

"Oh, him," I said, flabbergasted.

Huovinen's glee intensified.

"So was he drunk, then?"

"No. He just didn't want to be seen in the company of a cop. He's a gray-zone guy, one of my best informants. I'm going to tell the same story if the case goes anywhere. I got another piece of good news, too: that lady withdrew her extortion complaint. So I'm looking like a pretty clean-cut kid."

"What do you say, Ari?" Huovinen asked me.

"Sure."

"But the school of hard knocks did teach me that I'm going to spend less time fiddling around with cars and quit looking for thingamajigs while I'm on the clock. I also apologize for all of the inappropriate things I called you."

Oksanen's expression was so apologetic that I had to laugh. "When are you coming back to work? I could use you."

"It feels like my back pain and burnout just ended. How about tomorrow?"

"That's settled, then," Huovinen said, standing up.

"I have a work-related matter I need to talk to you about. I couldn't just kick back and relax totally," Oksanen said, following me. "I met with that guy, the heir who got into a legal battle with the foundation."

"The foundation?"

"The B. E. Kajasto Foundation, the one that donated over thirty million markkas to the Daybreak Academy. Son's name is Leif Kajasto. Lives in Vantaa and works at the airport fire station."

"Let's step into my office."

Once inside, we continued.

"I'd left him a message to call, and he did. So of course I went to meet him. We hit it off. Leif told me his pops had transferred his whole fortune to the foundation, more or less, after which the foundation's rules had been changed so that the real estate and wealth owned by the foundation would be used solely to support and develop Daybreak's activities. The board got to decide how the funds would be used. Two weeks after the old man made the will, he died in a car crash. The car was being driven by Sandberg, the foundation's CFO, who had also been elected to the board."

"Wow," I gasped.

"Then Leif was called in to work because some alarm light had come on during an incoming passenger flight. We agreed that next time we met, I'd bring the boss along."

"Fantastic."

"Should I set something up right now?"

I nodded.

Oksanen tapped at his phone and assumed a relaxed position. "Hey, Leif. Oksanen from Homicide here. You in a bad spot? You said we could meet again and I could bring my boss along. When do you have time?… Good, wait a sec, I'll ask my boss. What works for you?" Oksanen asked me.

"Whenever."

"Whenever, we could come right now… right on, we'll head over in a sec."

We met at the café at the airport service station. It was popular among cab drivers waiting for their shifts to start.

Leif Kajasto showed up in his firefighter's uniform. He was a big man, a little over fifty, who looked as if he'd taken his share of Antabuse courses and had just as many ahead. His skin was blotchy and his eyes were watery.

Oksanen stood to shake his hand. I stood up, too.

"I gave my boss a little bit of background. You can tell him the rest."

"Promise me you'll put those Holy Roller frauds up against the wall."

"Absolutely," Oksanen promised glibly.

Kajasto started off by telling us a little about his father. The old man had grown up the heir to a large farm and had made his fortune off of land and real-estate deals, then invested his money in ships. The war and fear of death had made him turn to God. When he was at the front, he promised that if he were allowed to live, he'd dedicate the majority of his wealth to doing good to his fellow man. He miraculously survived an intense artillery barrage, so after the war ended he made good on his promise. He set up a foundation in his own name that focused primarily on funding youth outreach and paying for the education of underprivileged youths. The old man didn't pull back from his business activities, either; he just kept getting richer. In the mid-1970s, after being diagnosed with lung cancer, he decided to focus on his spiritual work. That's when he found the Church of the Redemption, whose worldview matched his own. Around the same time, he had a falling-out with his only son, Leif.

"Dad wanted me to go to high school at Daybreak. I had zero interest in moving to the countryside. All my buddies lived in Helsinki. I dropped out after junior high and went to vocational school. That was the last straw for Dad. He wanted me to study economics or theology; there were no other alternatives. After school I worked a few years down at the shipyards. Then I applied to a firefighting course the City of Helsinki had organized. Dad wrote me off."

"Do you suspect anything fishy about your dad's death?" I asked.

"I'm not going to go and to say so publicly. Dad would have died of cancer within a few years anyway, but the way everything went down was a little too convenient for Daybreak. After that, no one came around telling them how to spend their money."

"Didn't the foundation's board monitor expenditures?"

"The guidelines were so vague and the board consisted of Sandberg, who was CFO at the time, Daybreak's

217

headmaster, a staff representative from Daybreak, a lawyer named Henry Silén, and some reverend from the Church of the Redemption."

"Do you remember the teacher's name?"

"Kärki, Särki…"

"Särkijärvi."

"That's the guy."

"As his son, you should have been entitled to your legally mandated share of the inheritance."

"Should have, if there had *been* an inheritance. Dad's wealth had gradually been shifted over to the foundation. By the time he died, all he had was the farm in Mäntyharju, the apartment in Helsinki, and a few hundred thousand in his bank account. The farm was willed to the church as a youth camp. I got the apartment."

"How big was his estate?"

"A cautious estimate would be at least thirty to forty million markkas. I got pissed off and hired a lawyer who had a reputation as a real shark. He requested a police investigation for embezzlement, because in his view Silén, whom the foundation had named as investment adviser, had invested a significant portion of the money contrary to my father's instructions. Three of the city's most ruthless attorneys were facing off there, and you can guess how that ended. My lawyer withdrew the request for investigation, I got a million marks for my pain and suffering, he billed me a hundred grand, and the foundation got to keep the rest. Last I heard, the money is long gone. Not too many pennies went to their intended purpose."

"Who were these three ruthless attorneys?"

"My lawyer was Veikko Ojanne, already dead and gone. Daybreak's investment adviser was a lawyer, the Henry Silén I was just talking about. His attorney was Heikki Moisio. A complete scumbag. I would have punched his lights out if I'd had the chance. Moisio's dead, too. I heard he was a junkie who talked too much about a client. There was an article about Silén a couple months ago in the paper. Said he'd mysteriously disappeared. Someone suspected that he skipped town after losing his own money, along with his clients'. I wouldn't be surprised."

"Have you seen any of the parties involved since then?"

"No... except Daybreak's headmaster at the time called me a few years ago. Someone had sent him a threatening letter. He thought it was me."

Oksanen chuckled. "Was it?"

"Nah."

"You don't know any former students from Daybreak?"

"Nope."

"Does the name the Brotherhood of the Sacred Vault say anything to you?"

"No. Sounds like rappers or something. Now you guys fill me in a little; tell me why you're interested in such an old case?"

"The names of several former Daybreak students have come up in conjunction with a certain investigation. We suspect the motive for the crime might lead back to Daybreak, in the late '70s."

"Sounds interesting. Tell me all about it once you solve the case… We can get together again, this time over a few cold ones."

"Offer noted," Oksanen said.

Oksanen lived on the way, so I promised to drop him off. He seemed to be in a reflective mood. The mental state did Oksanen good.

"Could you ask your contact at the *Helsingin Sanomat* for a clipping from the archives?"

"How old is the case?"

"Three years, give or take."

"No worries. That means it's in the digital archives, so it won't take more than a few seconds to get it. The old stories are stored in paper format in a different archive. They're harder to get your hands on."

I gave Oksanen the details of the story I was interested in, and he promised to deliver me an archive copy the next day. As he was getting out of the car outside his house, he suddenly froze. "I lost a lot of sleep thinking about all the bullshit I said, and I was sober, too."

Oksanen's wandering, regretful eyes placated me for good. "Let's agree that's ancient history." I slapped him on the shoulder and he climbed out of the car. He stood there uncertainly for a second, then headed towards his gate.

23

I almost felt a malicious glee when Headmaster Hätönen called me two days later, humbled and fearful. His explanations meandered, but the gist of his call was that Vesa Särkijärvi had been abducted.

I posed my own question in reply: "What makes you think that?"

"He boarded a flight to Helsinki two days ago and still hasn't accepted or answered any of my calls. He made a hotel reservation but never showed up. His wife is calling me in a panic, because he was supposed to have checked in with her that night."

"He's a grown man. Maybe he wandered off the straight and narrow... or bumped into an old friend and went to his place instead. A couple of drinks is all it takes to make people forget their promises."

"No, it's not. We were supposed to meet in Helsinki today and go through his speech."

"I'm sure you're aware that it's not possible to report an adult missing on the basis of such a brief disappearance."

"You suspected yourself that someone might be threatening him."

"I never said that."

"That's the impression I got from your questions. He also had a very important meeting at the EU offices in Helsinki. He never showed up there, either. In the era of modern technology, a person of Särkijärvi's stature can't just disappear unless something has happened to him."

I was starting to believe Hätönen was right, but it was better to let his panic grow before offering a helping hand. The more freaked out he was, the more he would talk.

"Is that a fact? I wonder who could possibly have been threatening him, and why?"

"A man in his station inevitably has enemies."

"I don't understand. He's an EU bureaucrat. Who hates them, except for Finnish nationalists?"

"That Laurén you're looking for hates him, for one."

"Why?"

"He and Särkijärvi had some conflict back at Daybreak."

"Are you talking about the instance where Särkijärvi molested him in your presence but you didn't dare to act as a witness on his behalf?"

"Apparently you take everything Laurén says at face value."

"I heard this from both Halme and Laurén's ex-wife. According to them, everyone knew Särkijärvi was a pedophile."

"So you're going to ignore my request based on slander. I thought the police do everything in their power to protect the public."

"Get back to me if Särkijärvi doesn't show up in a couple of days."

"I'm just trying to imagine how you'll explain it to your superiors and the media if it turns out he's been killed and you've given the criminal a two-day head start."

"Based on what you've told me, it's pretty hard to believe Särkijärvi has been abducted, let alone killed."

"You could at least find out where Laurén is."

"We've been trying to do that for the past week. You weren't particularly helpful in that endeavor."

"I apologize if that's the impression I gave. Ask whatever you want."

"We know what Särkijärvi has done. Does he have other enemies, aside from Laurén?"

"Halme promised to thrash Särkijärvi once when he was drunk, but Laurén's psychological problems are of such a nature that he might pose a genuine threat."

"A person like Särkijärvi might have more recent enemies. Well, I'll talk to my superior and see what we can do."

"Feel free to call anytime, day or night."

"Let me know if Särkijärvi emerges from his hiding place."

"Of course."

I went to report Särkijärvi's disappearance to Huovinen. I was headed back to my office when I got a call from the lobby informing me I had a visitor named Mandi Laurén. I turned right around and went downstairs.

Mandi rushed up and asked in a panic: "Do you know where my dad is?"

"No, unfortunately. I'm doing my best to find out, though."

"He's not responding, even to my emergency signal. He gave me a special password to use if I have to get in touch with him. He didn't answer."

"When was the last time you were in touch with your father?"

"Day before last. He said he might be hard to get hold of for a little while, but he would call me every day, or at least send a text message."

"So last time we met, you lied when you told me you hadn't been in touch with him?"

"Of course. He's my dad."

"Did you know he was staying in a cottage in Marjaniemi?"

"Yes."

"His classmate from Daybreak was shot in the vicinity of the cottage. Did you know about that?"

"Kai Halme. I heard about it. He was one of Dad's best friends. I liked him."

"Even though he seduced your mom."

Mandi grunted. "Dad always said he couldn't help it; it was his nature."

"If you want us to find your dad, there's something I need to know."

"What?"

"What was he planning on doing at the academy's centennial?"

"He was going to expose the bad things the teachers and administration had done. He always said he wouldn't be able to get over his past until he set the record straight with Daybreak. He was afraid he'd go crazy otherwise."

"How was he planning on doing that?"

"I can't tell you. If nothing's happened to him, he's still going to do it. It's nothing criminal."

"He's collaborating with that reporter, Moisio, isn't he?"

The look on Mandi's face told me I was right.

"I'm going to tell you something I really shouldn't. The man your dad is planning on taking vengeance on is a former teacher at the academy, Vesa Särkijärvi. He's missing, too. He's been gone for two days, like your dad. Do you know anything about that?"

"No. I know the name and what he did, that's all."

"Could your dad have anything to do with the disappearance?"

"I know how he's going to get back at him. Dad would never kidnap or kill anyone, not even that pig."

"I believe you. Do you know what kind of car your dad is driving?"

"A silver Citroën wagon. It's in Kai Halme's name."

I was caught off guard. Halme had really pulled the wool over our eyes. An edgier man than I expected had been hiding under the bank manager's slick exterior.

"Do you have any thoughts about what might have happened to your father? Do you know something? Is that why you're so worried?"

Mandi looked at her shoes for a moment.

"Dad said a week ago that he might be in danger. He's never said anything like that before. I'm positive he's not making it up."

"Did he tell you what the danger was?"

"I asked him, but he said he didn't want to put me in harm's way, and that's why he wouldn't tell me."

"He must have said something more than that."

"All he said was that he had realized something and that if his suspicions were right, he might be in danger. But he promised to let me know one way or the other if his suspicions got stronger…" Mandi wiped the corner of her eye. "I'm positive something bad has happened to my dad."

"I'll do what I can to help, but your dad isn't an easy man to find."

"The one thing I do know is that Dad isn't in Helsinki; he's somewhere in the countryside."

"How do you know that?"

"He said he'd be in touch at the latest the minute he gets back into town. I felt like he was with someone and was calling so the other person wouldn't hear. He was lowering his voice that way."

"Are you sure there's nothing else you can do to help us?" I asked as I walked her out. "We need all the help we can get."

She momentarily withdrew into her shell, then reached into her purse and handed me a CD.

"Ola and I made this. It's from an old cassette tape; we filtered out the background noise and copied it onto CD. If Dad's OK, I've made a huge mistake, but I'll make an even bigger one if I don't give this to you and something happens to him."

I accepted the CD and thanked her.

Mandi wiped her eyes. "Dad said that when his soul is at peace, he'll buy a house in the countryside and start growing carrots and onions and take me with him. A dad like that can't be bad... can he?"

"Absolutely not," I said.

I watched Mandi hurry off. For a second, it felt like I'd missed out on something.

I returned to my office, closed the door behind me, inserted the CD into a laptop, and put on my headphones. I grabbed the mouse and clicked Play. The first thing I heard was the sound of a metal door closing. Next, I heard a distinct hum in the background, as if some big machine had started up. Then I heard a voice. From what I could make out, I decided the person talking was a young man standing a few yards from the tape recorder.

"*What are you hiding in the corner for? You don't have to be afraid. We're buddies, aren't we? Aren't we?*"

The reply, in a boy's voice, was listless: "*I guess. But I still have to go to bed. It's already lights out and everyone else is in bed.*"

"*Don't worry about that. I'm the monitor and decide who gets to do what and when. You're with me. Plus, you're my friend, aren't you, Reijo?*" The man's voice was cajoling and demanding at the same time. "*Come here, right next to me. Now.*"

A clunk and hesitant footsteps.

"*Stand right there and look me in the eyes, not at the floor.*"

227

A tinny sound, as if someone had struck a big metal kettle with a stick.

"*I said, there. Now.*"

A moment's silence. Then the boy's teary voice. "*I'm really tired and my stomach hurts... I wanna go to bed —*"

"*Didn't I give you a big chocolate bar and other cool stuff today? Isn't that the way it's supposed to be, friends do nice things for their friends, things that feel good? You get chocolate and I get something else. What's wrong with that?*"

No answer. The sound of rustling clothes and a metallic clang.

"*The door's locked. There's no point trying to go anywhere. We're the only ones here and no one's going to hear you, no matter how loud you shout. Let's just be nice to each other and then you can go to bed.*"

"*I don't want to, why do I have to —*"

"*You have to because I say so.*"

"*What if I tell my dad —*"

"*I'll tell you what I'll do if you even hint at anything... I'll get Anteroinen and we'll come get you one night, tie you up, and throw you in this boiler. There won't be anything left of you but some burnt bits of bone. Now stop bawling and pull down your pants...*"

I pressed Stop and tried to remember who had told me about the tape recording. I stared at the ceiling for a few minutes, and then I remembered.

24

Oksanen was like a new man. He was bursting with enthusiasm when he brought in the article I'd requested, which he'd picked up early that morning from the *Helsingin Sanomat* offices on his way in.

"Is it the right one?" he asked, eyeing the story. It was a full-page article in *Ilta-Sanomat* about crime on the Costa del Sol. The story included interviews with the NBI's narcotics contacts in Malaga and a few Finns who had lived in Fuengirola for a long time. Burglaries and robberies had exploded, primarily committed by drug users and Yugoslavian, Bulgarian, Romanian, and Russian criminals. Many Finns who had moved to Spain to spend their retirement days in the sun had packed up their things and gone back to Finland.

"Yup. Thanks. Don't go anywhere for an hour. I'll ask Huovinen if he can make it to a last-minute meeting."

"I'll be here like a bump on a log," Oksanen promised.

I took a stack of paper from the printer and started formulating my thoughts, writing down five names in a vertical timeline. At the top of the list came Kivalo, who died first, then Sandberg, who died second; third was our dearly departed Anteroinen, then Heikki Moisio, and then at the bottom of the list the most recent victim, Halme. Underneath them, I wrote three more names: Silén, Särkijärvi, Laurén. After each of them I wrote a question mark.

I flipped through my notes until I found Detective Rimpelä's number and called.

"You guys solve Anteroinen's murder?" he asked in a malicious tone.

"Not yet, but as it just so happens that's who I'm calling about. You told me he was facing charges in some major theft ring. Do you know who his attorney was?"

"Sure. I've never met such a huge asshole in my life. Blamed the police for his client's death. Claimed the investigators had intentionally leaked information about Anteroinen's being an informant and that's why he was killed. Threatened to file a complaint with the ombudsman. I told him he could complain to Mother Amma for all I cared."

"The name?"

"Moisio, Heikki Moisio."

Now I had all the pieces of the puzzle in my hands, it was time to start putting them together. I had been fingering some of the pieces throughout the entire investigation without coming up with the right places for them. Now that I'd found the missing ones, the rest fell into position. The image grew sharper and sharper, and the end was a cinch.

I called Huovinen then and there. "I think the case is starting to come together. When can you meet?"

"How about right now?"

25

The cars parked outside Daybreak indicated that the academy counted some extremely successful men and women among its former students. I saw a slew of black Mercedes, big, gleaming silver Audis, Volvos emanating middle-class security. Japanese vehicles were in the minority.

Guests dressed to the nines were crowded outside the main door, along with a few students in more mundane gear having a smoke. People were shaking hands as they searched through the decades for that old classmate they could barely recognize. The most successful didn't take long to find each other; the less successful hung back uncertainly.

I saw Headmaster Hätönen speaking with a man in a suit, by all appearances a high-level civil servant. Then a Ministry of Education vehicle pulled up, and Hätönen rushed over to greet this even more prestigious guest, a broad smile on his face. He took the minister's hand in both of his and said something clearly intended to amuse, because the minister laughed stiffly.

"Headmaster Hätönen," I said to Simolin.

Moisio was standing off to the side, accompanied by his photographer. He saw me, made some remark to the photographer, and started heading over. The photographer followed a moment later, camera at the ready.

I continued coaching Simolin: "Moisio from *Ilta-Sanomat*."

"I recognized him."

"What are the police hoping to find here?" the journalist said, attempting a light-hearted smile.

"What about a crime reporter? Crimes don't happen in places like this."

"Big fish swim in still waters…"

"You know exactly why we're here. We'd like to talk to Särkijärvi, too, but apparently he's canceled."

The photographer was standing behind Moisio, ready for action, and heard what I said. "He's not coming?"

"I guess not."

"Where the fuck are we going to get pictures for the story, then?"

"Get some shots of the buildings and the visitors. That'll be enough. We'll drop in an official headshot of Särkijärvi," the reporter said.

The minister found someone else to talk to, and Hätönen approached us with clipped steps. He was wearing a dark suit and a steel-blue tie, and his face was flushed with big-day excitement.

"So Särkijärvi's not coming?" he asked, voice dripping with accusation.

"He still hasn't gotten in touch with you?"

"Not a word, and we can't reach him. His wife and family are very concerned. In my view, the police have acted extremely recklessly in this instance —"

"We've done everything in our power."

"Is Särkijärvi missing?" the reporter asked, pulling out his notebook. The photographer immediately zoomed in on Hätönen.

"Could we have a word in my office?" Hätönen said, shooing away the photographer.

"I guess you're not going to get your scoop after all," I said to Moisio.

He chuckled. "The story's ready. We just wanted a photo and a little ambiance, and comments from the minister and maybe a couple of former students."

"I'd love to read the article before it's published; to check the facts, you know," Hätönen said. "I still don't understand what the story is. The story, if you can even call it one, is over twenty years old."

"Many of the guilty parties and those in positions of responsibility continue to hold important roles in society. Like Särkijärvi. We have extremely damaging evidence on him."

"Well, there's no need for a gossip-rag reporter to ask me any questions, then," Hätönen snapped, and made for the building. On the way, he noticed a man climbing out of a black car and turned towards this new arrival with his hand raised. I recognized the man as the traitorous bishop Laurén had cursed, Johan Kaltio. Hätönen immediately led him inside, gesticulating in my direction. Maybe he was afraid I would arrest his prominent guest.

"I think we'll get out of here, too. I look forward to the story. I have nothing against someone writing about it; on the contrary."

I took a couple of steps, but then turned around. "Do you happen to know where Laurén is? He was supposed to execute some sort of ambush here today."

"We were supposed to meet here this morning, but he's not answering my calls."

"Hopefully Särkijärvi's and Laurén's disappearances aren't connected to each other."

"I'm sure they're not."

"How are you so sure?"

"Because everything was so carefully planned."

"What was supposed to take place here today?"

"A minor provocation, harmless but embarrassing for a lot of people. We're going to conjure up the ghosts of the past."

"When was the last time you spoke with Laurén?"

"Yesterday. I don't get why he's not here. I can do the story without him, but I've been counting on what we agreed."

"Let me know if you hear from him. It's for his own good, too."

"So you guys are giving up already?"

"I have better things to do. We've arranged for a local police patrol to hang around just in case. Remember that charges of aiding and abetting are likelier than you think."

Moisio laughed nonchalantly. He put his trust in his newspaper's prominence, their crackerjack legal team, and the police's desire to maintain good relations with the mainstream media. And he wasn't completely off base.

"What now?" Simolin asked, once we were in the car.

"Now we wait."

Three hours later we were still waiting.

We were in a gray corrugated metal warehouse; a heap of machines whose purpose was obscure to me stood at the far end. From the dust and the junk, car tires, plastic containers, and pallets tossed on top of them, you could tell they hadn't been used for years. Up against the wall there was a metal box at least six feet tall with a large electric motor on the side. I couldn't figure out what it had been used for. The warehouse only had a few smutty windows that the gray spring light listlessly tried to penetrate. I peered out of one and looked around. Across from the warehouse there was a broad open space, crossed by a row of low-slung sheds, each about fifty yards long. Birch saplings dotted the yard, and a broken-down yellow tractor had been left to rust at the rear. It crouched lopsidedly in the brush, as if embarrassed by its abject state. A field loomed in the distance, and beyond it, black spruce woods.

In the other direction, at the edge of the open space, stood a flat-roofed, '60s brick home with an incongruous wooden extension. Someone had had more money than taste. Based on how overgrown the garden was, it had also been left to its own devices.

A tall chain-link fence stood between the house and the warehouse. There was no movement anywhere.

Simolin circled the warehouse and picked up something from the ground, then carried it over for me to inspect. It was a tin can, pea soup, full of holes.

"Shot through with a rifle or a pistol."

"We'll look for the shells later."

Simolin continued exploring the area. It wasn't long before I got tired of sitting there and started poking around too. A couple of old wooden doors were leaning against the wall, along with a few sheets of the corrugated metal used to roof the warehouse. I peeked behind the sheets and spied something white in the gloom. I moved the sheets aside, and saw a door with an unusual metal handle.

"There's a cold store here," I shouted to Simolin, who came over, his curiosity piqued.

"They must have kept the feed frozen," Simolin mused.

I opened the door. Darkness and stale air punched me in the face.

Simolin came up behind me and pointed his flashlight in. The room was about ten by ten feet. I could make out a stack of plastic containers that looked like white moving boxes. In the corner there were a few pallets on wheels, a swiveling office chair, and a desk lying on its side. That was all I could see, but I stepped in regardless. Metal tracks ran across the ceiling, with steel hooks hanging from them.

Simolin kicked the wall. It echoed dully. "Steel." He let the beam from the flashlight sweep across the floor.

"Someone's been here. There's no dust." He was right; the floor looked freshly swept.

The flashlight beam climbed up the wall to the ceiling.

"Stop!" I ordered. "Keep it on the track."

Simolin obeyed, and I stepped closer. My fingers reached up and came into contact with something.

"What is it?"

I studied my find. It was a tightly folded piece of paper the size of a postage stamp. I unfolded it.

A SIM card. I examined the paper. There was a four-digit number on it.

I turned off my phone, removed the battery, switched out my SIM card for the one I'd found, then turned my phone back on. A second later it asked for my PIN code. I entered the number from the slip of paper. The phone unlocked.

I copied the contacts from the SIM card to my phone. There were a few dozen. I recognized several of them, including my own.

"Must be from Laurén's phone."

"Strange place to hide it," Simolin remarked.

I switched it back out for my own SIM card. After inspecting the other tracks without finding anything, we went back into the warehouse.

"Let's go over to the house."

We had gotten in through the chain-link fence at a spot where it had collapsed. It looked as if a car or tractor had crashed into one of the poles, knocking it over at ground level. It was possible to lift the fence free at the pole and slip under it.

Our car was parked just outside. We drove over to the house, which was surrounded by a dilapidated white wooden fence that a solid kick would have knocked over. A path of concrete pavers led to the front door.

I received a succinct text message: *Coming!*

"He's coming," I said to Simolin.

Five minutes later, we saw a cloud of dust at the end of the road, followed by the vehicle that was kicking it up. A moment later, I could tell the car's make and color.

It was a dark green Range Rover. It seemed to be accelerating, as if the driver were in a hurry to find out what we were up to. The vehicle parked a few yards away. The windows were tinted, so we couldn't see who was driving, but I knew who it was.

Moisio stepped out, looking irate. "What are you doing here?" he demanded.

"Was it a good party?" I asked.

"A bunch of bullshit speeches." The reporter leaned against his Range Rover and stared at me.

"Oh, what are we doing here? We're looking for Laurén."

"Here? Why?"

"Because his cell-phone signal was most recently picked up nearby, through a base station located a mile from here, to be exact, and because you conveniently happened to have a farm you inherited in the vicinity. We decided to check if you've been putting him up."

"I haven't."

"You don't mind if we have a look around, do you? We could use a cup of coffee, too."

"You better bet I mind. And you can get coffee from the gas station in town… The thing is, I use this house as an off-site office. I've got source-protected material spread around in there."

"We're not interested in your material. You can cover it up; take your time."

"Sorry, it's still not going to work."

The reporter tapped at his phone and reached someone: "Hey Markku, you have a minute? I've got a bit of an unusual situation here. I just arrived at my farm and there's a detective here who wants to search the premises. I've got source-protected journalistic material spread around in there, because I'm doing that story on Daybreak for next week's issue, and I have no intention of letting them in. Would you mind having a word with the esteemed lieutenant?" He handed me the phone.

"What's going on there?" It was Pyysalo, *Ilta-Sanomat*'s legal counsel, trying to sound all businesslike and worth his considerable salary.

"We're looking for an individual who's got an APB out on him. He's been in contact with Moisio and was traced here."

"Traced how?"

"Some pretty incredible technology: via Laurén's phone. We have reason to suspect Moisio is hiding him. He's preventing us from searching the place, which of course increases our suspicions."

"So you don't have a search warrant?"

"I'm the lead investigator and as such have the authority to order a house search whenever I want. But an honest

journalist can't have anything to hide. We're not looking for porn magazines, and we're not trying to expose
anyone who's leaking information. We're investigating
several homicides."

"Is Laurén suspected of these homicides?"

"Among other things."

"Would you please hand the phone back to Moisio?"

I gave the phone back.

"Yes... of course it is... I see this as an attempt to get
around source protection; it's an outrageous violation...
I could, but I don't want to. The police can't just march
into a newspaper's editorial offices to conduct a search
either."

"You better believe we can," I interjected.

"Couldn't you get in touch with the lawyer at the
Union of Journalists? I'm sure they'd be interested...
yeah, just a sec... Pyysalo wants to talk to you again."

"Have you considered that what we're talking about
here are core journalistic values? The media is going to
have it in for you. The new Minister of Justice has been
stressing freedom of the press and its significance in a
democracy. I suggest you drop it this time. I spoke with
Moisio; he says he wants to do everything he can to help
you —"

"Moisio's resistance has heightened my suspicions that
he's hiding critical investigative information from us, so
I've decided we'll be conducting an immediate search
of the premises. Moisio is under arrest for the duration."

Pyysalo made a last-ditch effort: "Are you sure you've
given all the ramifications sufficient consideration?"

"Far too much." I ended the call. "You heard what I said."

The reporter decided it was wisest to give in. "Why don't I show you around? What do you want to see?"

"We don't need a native guide. If we need your help, we'll ask for it. Wait here in your car while we have a look around." I held out my hand. "I'll take your phone until we're done." Moisio was forced to restrain himself. "And the keys to the house."

Once they were turned over to us, Simolin and I entered the premises.

The house didn't smell as stale as I'd expected; someone had been there recently. And I knew the journalist had come straight from Helsinki.

It was a single-story house without a basement. There were half a dozen rooms; it didn't take long for us to go through them. Then we sat down in the living room to kill time. I made a couple of calls. After chatting together for fifteen minutes, Simolin and I went back outside. Moisio was sitting obediently in his car. He stepped out when he saw us.

"Well, did you find anything?"

"What should I have found?"

"What are you looking for?"

"All kinds of stuff."

"You mind if I get to work now? I have an eight o'clock deadline."

"The search is just ramping up. This is a big place. That's why we called in backup: more men and a couple of tracking dogs."

"You can't be serious."

"You better believe we are."

My phone rang. I didn't recognize the number, but I recognized the voice. It was Deputy National Police Commissioner Arto Kalliola.

"What the hell are you doing, Kafka? I have the editor-in-chief and lawyer from *Ilta-Sanomat* breathing down my neck. Then the ministry's permanent secretary called."

"Normal investigative work. House search."

"Searching a journalist's house is not normal, even for you."

"We suspect a serious crime."

"What is this supposed serious crime?"

"Are five murders enough for you?"

Kalliola lost it. "What the hell are you talking about?"

A five-car convoy approached the house.

"I don't have time to talk. We want to search the area as thoroughly as possible before nightfall."

"I hope you're not putting your career on the line. This is all on you, and you alone."

We stepped outside to meet the cars. The first was Oksanen's Audi; Stenman was sitting in the passenger seat. It was followed by two unmarked cars, a marked police Mondeo, and a police van. Moisio gaped at the incursion in shock.

"Put him in the van to wait," I ordered.

"You want us to cuff him?" the uniformed driver asked eagerly.

"Knock yourself out."

The reporter was about to explode. He stared at the handcuffs as if he couldn't believe his eyes.

Oksanen and Stenman headed off with one of the patrols to inspect the warehouse; Simolin led a second patrol into the house. I stayed back with the dog handlers to negotiate the search. One of the cadaver dogs headed into the forest behind the house. Another went to search the warehouse and the cold store. I stayed in my vehicle to report to Huovinen and ponder my next move.

I was climbing out of the car when I noticed a silver Golf approaching the property; it parked in the yard a moment later. The photographer I'd seen in Moisio's company at Daybreak stepped out, camera aimed and ready.

"What's going on here? The editor-in-chief called and told me to come get some photos."

"This is a crime scene. If you want to photograph, go back to the road, unless you want to end up in the cell next to Moisio."

The photographer aimed the camera at my face.

"You can tell me what's going on, can't you?"

"It's confidential information under investigative powers legislation."

"Come on, now you're fucking with me. I'm just doing my job."

"So am I."

The photographer gave up and retreated to the road. He switched the lens out for a telephoto and kept it trained on the property.

"Ari!" Stenman shouted from the warehouse doorway. She waved, and I walked over. "Jari found something."

Oksanen was up on top of the big steel container next to the wall. He scanned the insides of the box one last time before climbing down the ladder fixed to the side. "I found this." He handed me a gleaming golden nugget the size of a pea.

I studied it more closely and almost dropped it.

"A gold tooth. Found it at the bottom of the feed mill."

26

Moisio stared at the tooth I was holding between my thumb and forefinger. He struggled to remain expressionless, but a tremor in his cheek muscles revealed it wasn't easy. "What is it?"

"A gold tooth. According to the missing person report, Silén had a gold tooth. We'll compare this to his dental X-rays. The tooth was in the feed mill. We also found this." Now I showed him the SIM card we'd found.

The photographer tried to move in, but I ordered the patrol to chase him off and one of the men to keep an eye on him.

"Laurén's SIM card. It was in the cold store. We'll use it to trace his calls and movements. I'm sure you know what comes next. I'll call in more backup, and we'll cordon off the whole area and have the cadaver dogs go over every square inch. There's always some trace, no matter how careful you are. The technical investigators will scour the mill and the rest of the warehouse. I'm sure we'll find Silén's and Laurén's DNA. Pretty soon media from around the country will be here. There'll be television cameras and helicopters. The reporters will set up camp outside your gate and watch the place 24/7. Your face is going to be on every TV screen in the country. Make no mistake, your pack is going to turn on you."

My performance was so commanding that Moisio backed up until he was sitting in the doorway of the van. He only had one card left to play, and I knew what it was. Covering his face with his hands, he shook his head, and said in a quivering voice: "I had to… it was horrible. I'd never have believed Laurén was capable of it. He always told me you had to love evildoers, too, and he'd get his revenge by playing that tape through the intercom speakers during Särkijärvi's speech, that's all. We decided I would do a story on it. That would have been the end of Särkijärvi's career. The police were looking for Laurén, and he didn't have anyplace to go. So I promised he could use this place until the centennial; I only come here a few times a year. And it's near Daybreak. I believed everything he told me —"

"Are you telling me Laurén killed Silén and Särkijärvi?"

"It was like I was in the middle of a nightmare. When I came here yesterday, there was no one in the house, but I heard the feed mill running. They used to use it to grind up slaughterhouse scraps for mink and fox feed. When I opened the door, I saw Laurén standing next to the mill, and it was running. There were a bunch of plastic containers next to it full of human…"

I saw Oksanen scowl in disbelief. "You're saying he turned those guys into hamburger?"

"When Laurén noticed me, he realized he'd been caught, grabbed the knife, and started coming at me. I knew he'd kill me if I didn't... The old pistol Dad used to use to put down sick foxes was hanging there in the warehouse; I snatched it, and when Laurén rushed me I started shooting. The bullet hit him in the head and he died instantly."

Moisio fell silent. I saw his shoulders quivering. It was a convincing performance.

"What did you do with the bodies?"

"I knew right away that no one would believe me, least of all the police. I didn't have a choice —"

"So Laurén is also..."

The reporter's silence was the answer.

"Where are they?"

The answer was almost swallowed up in the din of a helicopter diving over the field. The photographer was hanging out the door, shooting rapid-fire at us.

"I dug a hole in the woods and..."

27

Sitting in the car, I watched the landscape glide past, the dark flanks of the spruce woods, the dreary clay fields that went on for miles.

I wouldn't have been able to take bright spring sun at the moment anyway. I'd solved the case, but I had solved it too late. Thanks to my sluggish brain, three people were dead. I didn't mourn Särkijärvi or Silén, but Laurén was a different story. In the end, he was the only one who had dared to take action. On top of that, I'd promised Mandi I would look after her father. Thinking about that chilled me, and guilt stabbed me in the back. I was afraid to even think about seeing Mandi.

After getting too stuck on the theory of Laurén's vengeance, I had dismissed the motivation that has generated the most violence and suffering throughout the centuries: greed. The killer hadn't acted out of vengeance, but to get his hands on the foundation's millions.

This seed of greed had been sown back when the older Moisio brother had taken Silén on as a client during the foundation's battle over Kajasto's inheritance. He had discovered that the money was kept in several overseas accounts and the investments were all a sham. The seed had germinated when Moisio had taken on Silén's fraud case ten years later. While handling the recused Silén's financial affairs, Moisio had learned that the money was in a joint account held by Silén and Särkijärvi; Särkijärvi had one of the account numbers, and Silén had the other. Any withdrawals and transfers required both of them. The members of the foundation's board had all been bought off or intimidated into silence. Kivalo was given an apartment in Spain; Sandberg got a seaside house in Kotka.

Moisio told his reporter brother about the money, at which point they decided to heist it together.

Their first bit of business was silencing anyone who knew about it. The younger brother traveled to Spain to do a story on Finns and crime on the Costa del Sol. During that trip he killed Kivalo. Soon after, they drowned Sandberg together.

When he heard about the deaths, Särkijärvi realized they couldn't be a coincidence. He initially suspected Silén, which was why he recruited Anteroinen to be his bodyguard. Anteroinen had been complicit in the incidents at Daybreak, and their shared pastime had forced the men into a relationship of mutual trust. But the Moisio brothers surprised Anteroinen and drowned him in the septic tank. The older brother thought he was being cute when he carved the symbol of the Brotherhood of the Sacred Vault into Anteroinen's back.

Now the only ones left were Särkijärvi and Silén.

The operation had suffered a momentary setback when the older brother was stabbed to death over complications with drug dealers. The little brother decided to soldier on regardless, because the goal and the prize were within reach.

Jyri Moisio had met Laurén at one of his brother's parties and was aware of his past. He decided to take advantage of Laurén's obsession with bringing Särkijärvi to justice. The job of crime reporter demanded contact with people like Laurén, so everything came together naturally.

Moisio understood that Daybreak's centennial would be the best moment to strike, because Särkijärvi would be coming to Finland. With that as a pretense, he'd also be able to steer Laurén at will, especially once he figured out how to use the old cassette recording.

The only risk was Laurén's increasing ungovernability. He came up with crazy ideas and wanted to lay the groundwork for his big reveal with acts that would guarantee media attention. Stealing his girlfriend's body and the funeral pyre were Laurén's ideas. Moisio was forced to help, but as a crime reporter, that was easy. He received praise from his superiors for his scoops and was ordered to follow the story more closely than ever. In the end, Laurén's antics proved to be an advantage. After the theft and subsequent burning of the body, the police wouldn't be surprised by anything Laurén did, even if he ended up killing Silén and Särkijärvi in a delusional state.

But Laurén had started to suspect Moisio's motives. His doubts were sparked when Moisio wasn't interested in writing about the foundation money the Academy had misappropriated, even though the topic should have interested him. Laurén had considered Kivalo's and Anteroinen's deaths acts of divine vengeance, but Silén's disappearance roused his suspicions. Halme's death opened his eyes completely. Halme had called Moisio and berated him for exploiting a sick man. He'd threatened to talk to the editor-in-chief the next day, and said he'd meet Laurén that same night and force him to turn himself in. That would have thrown Moisio's schemes into turmoil, because he needed Laurén as a scapegoat. In addition, if Laurén would have given himself up, the police might have squeezed information out of him that could lead the investigators onto his tracks. So Halme had to die.

Laurén immediately guessed who the killer was, because only Sotamaa, Mandi, and Moisio knew where he was holed up. And so he prepared for the worst by writing a long, detailed letter. Nevertheless, he decided to continue with the plan, damn the consequences.

Upon Särkijärvi's arrival in Finland, Moisio lured him to a meeting under the guise of an interview and abducted him. Silén had already been a prisoner for two months. Once he got both account numbers – he wouldn't kill Silén and Särkijärvi until he had them – he confirmed their authenticity by transferring a small sum. With both Silén and Särkijärvi locked in the cold store, he went off to pick up Laurén. It would be best if all three permanently disappeared.

Moisio asked Laurén to go with him to his farm, saying it was a safe place where they could work out the final preparations for exposing Daybreak. But on the way there, Laurén mailed the letter outlining his suspicions to his daughter. He instructed her to open it only if she didn't hear from him for two days. When the time was up, she came to me in tears: "You have to go there right away. They're going to kill Dad... and it's my fault, because I listened to him and waited."

She gave me the letter, from which I learned the rest, including the fact that Moisio would get life in prison. No one would believe his explanations.

The vista outside the window looked bleaker and bleaker, as was only fitting. I deserved it.

"I never would have believed Moisio would give up so easily," Simolin reflected. "I guess he realized we'd find the bodies anyway. Freshly dug holes aren't hard to find. He figured it was smarter to get there first and explain things away as best he could rather than wait for us to tell our own version of events."

"You've got to be kidding!" Stenman cried, staring at the laptop on her knees.

"What?" Simolin asked.

"*Ilta-Sanomat* already published a story on it: 'Fur farm frenzy: victims ground up in feed mill and buried in the woods.'"

Moisio got his scoop after all.